RESIST and
fight for your
right to be
Free.

Amy Hart

Resilience

surviving in the face of everything

a collection of work by (C)AMAB trans writers

Edited by Amy Heart,
Larissa Glasser, & Sugi Pyrrophyta

Heartspark Press
Olympia, WA

Heartspark Press
PO Box 1659
Olympia, WA 98501-1659

ISBN (hardback): 978-0-692-95108-8
ISBN (paperback): 978-0-9996730-0-3
Library of Congress Control Number: 2017914110

For commercial permissions, please address written requests to: hello@heartsparkpress.com.

If you're a TERF, don't bother asking. We won't say yes.

In loving memory of our fallen sisters in 2017

Alloura Wells
Ally Steinfeld
Alphonza Watson
Ava Le'Ray Barrin
Brian Fitzgerald Sherrell Faulkner
Brooklyn BreYanna Stevenson
Candace Towns
Chay Reed
Chyna Doll Dupree
Ciara McElveen
Derricka Banner
Ebony Morgan
Elizabeth Stephanie Montez
Gwynevere River Song
Hilario López Ruiz
Jamie Lee Wounded Arrow
Jaquarrius Holland
Jessica Rubi Mori
Jojo Striker
Kenne McFadden
Kendra Marie Adams
Kiwi Herring
Misty Garcia
Mesha Caldwell
Pepper "Phoenix" K
Sisi Thibert
Sherrell Faulkner
Scout Schultz
Tavita Montes
TeeTee Dangerfield
Tiara Lashaytheboss Richmond
Yadira

and to those who have never been heard
Rest in Power

Contents

This book is dedicated to all of the sweet gems
desperately searching for a roadmap in this
violent, transmisogynistic world.

May the stories written here
help you find your way back home.

Foreword
Julia Serano

Most stories about trans women focus almost entirely on our experiences with gender: When did we first realize that we wanted to be a girl? Did we prefer feminine clothes and toys, rather than doing things typically associated with boys? What were the various steps along our journeys of gender exploration that ultimately led us to identify as female? What physical and psychological changes did we experience during our transitions? Are we finally comfortable with our gender? What is it like now, to finally be a woman?

I, like many trans women past and present, often feel compelled to make my own personal story (or stories I create) fit into that traditional, gender-focused, narrative format. Unfortunately, this formula overlooks and obscures the countless ways in which our lives are shaped by being trans that have nothing to do with either our gender or identity. So, if you will, allow me to briefly tell a different rendition of my story.

At the age of eleven, I discovered something about myself. A secret. Or perhaps it was a riddle. Whatever it was, it was downright dangerous. It had the power to devastate my family, estrange my friends, and make me the target of ridicule and abuse. So I kept it to myself. At first, holding onto that secret was painful—worse than clinging onto a pot of boiling water. It often scalded me and scarred me, but I never let go. And over time, I learned something about myself: I was strong. I could endure anything. I was capable of persevering.

And this riddle that I uncovered defied common sense. It forced me to question all conventional wisdom. I started applying critical thinking, not just to this particular matter, but to everything in my purview. I carried out my own experiments, formed my own opinions, and relied on my own resourcefulness. I learned to listen to my own body and trust my own instincts. I cultivated open-mindedness and empathy toward other people because, for all I knew, they might be grappling with riddles and obstacles of their own.

1

For a few years, I did all of this in isolation. But eventually, after much searching, I found a community of people like me. We swapped stories and shared our ideas and theories with one another. We developed our own language and culture, and offered each other support and camaraderie. While each of us was formidable in our own right, together we were even stronger.

Eventually, I solved the riddle. The solution was to not keep it secret anymore. So I turned myself inside out for the entire world to see. Eleven-year-old me would have been scared to death by this prospect, but the interim years of questioning and persisting had made me confident and unashamed of who I was. Upon coming out, some people liked what they saw. Others expressed confusion, concern, or derision. There were countless barbs and insults directed at me—sometimes they'd sting briefly, but they were incapable of truly hurting me. Over the years, I had learned to love myself, believe in myself; no ignorant outsider could (or can) ever take that away from me.

Sometimes, upon discovering that I am trans, well-meaning acquaintances will say, "Wow, you're really courageous." Such remarks feel like a backhanded compliment, as they seem to suggest that being a trans woman is such a horrible fate that I must be brave simply for being one. In reality, I am proud of who I am and wouldn't trade my transgender experiences for anything. But on top of that, the notion that I must be "brave" or "courageous" rings false. It presumes that I had a choice in the matter. It implies that I was offered two possible paths, one risky and the other completely safe, and that I unflinchingly chose the former over the latter. But being trans was never a choice; it was inexplicably foisted upon me. And when you are transgender, there is no such thing as a safe path: You can be out or closeted, transition or not, but every available option is potentially perilous.

So rather than calling trans women "brave" or "courageous," I wish more people would see us for what we really are: *Resilient.*

AMAB (assigned male at birth) trans people, including trans women like me, vary in every possible way. We each have different histories, our lives follow different trajectories, and we have a myriad of different stories to tell. But the one thing that we all share is our resilience—our tenacity to survive and ability to thrive despite the relentless hostility, hurdles, and setbacks we face. Despite growing up in a world steeped in transphobia and misogyny, we have somehow managed to be true to ourselves and forge our own paths. We are resilient, and each and every story in this collection is a testament to that.

Black, Trans, and Still Breathing
KOKUMO

it all started in a slave-ship
the belly of a beast whose appetite your ancestors could neva' satisfy
but that didn't keep the behemoth from feeding
and after the ship shit out their remains
like a barn owl vomiting up the hair and bones of field mice
you
not willing to let go of the mortal coil reincarnated
then it all started on an auction block
ten feet from soil you just saw for the first time in your life
but could only grow to resent
you were sold before you even knew what day of the week it was
worked from when the moon
whispered until the sun screamed
and when its rays baked you like a pie left out on a kitchen ledge
you fell dead
but refusing to go before you manifested all you could
your soul remained on this realm
then it all started in a war
strange men told you your freedom was
finally of concern to them
and gave you a gun
it wasn't the best and neither were the clothes
but massa needed to be taught a lesson
and you would be damned if you died a slave
so bullets flew from your rifle tantamount to
Aladdin rubbing the genie's lamp
only these bullets weren't wishes but a declaration of independence
or so you thought
when the casualties were counted your corpse
was discovered amongst the heap
but your soul once again couldn't leave when
freedom had finally come knockin' on ya' door
so you gathered your resolve and gave life another chance

4

KOKUMO

to disappoint you
and that it did
then it all started up norf'
some place big
some place cold
some place fast enough to make you forget the
phantom pains those whippins' left
"a factory job ain't much different from pickin' tobacco", you said
"but at least dis' time you ain't gots' ta'
water the crops with your tears"
the unions weren't made fa' niggas
and they told you this every time you got ta' bankin' on a promise
quick to remind you that that
promise was made ta' white men n' not you
so they paid you less
told you ta' shut up
told you ta' stay in your place
n' be grateful they even let you sweep the floors
and you were
because at least up norf' the klan couldn't turn
your torched body into beef jerky
and pickle ya' dreams like a jar ah' hogmogs or pig's feet
but what you, didn't know
was that they traded them badges for sheets
once you crossed the Mason Dixon line
and the grand wizard became the chief of police
and the folks who'd rather hang you would
now prefer just ta' shoot you dead
but once again
not quite done birthing all of your prismatic-self
you came back to the third dimension
then it all started behind a picket line
dogs bittin' you like the bone nem' white folks jus' couldn't stop pickin'
wata' hoses louda' and stronga' than the ocean
ya' ancestors were forced to cross
you laid-up in that city street bloodied and

unconscious afta one too many billy clubs did you in
but wudn't a Molotov cocktail strong enough
to incinerate the glimmer of freedom in your heart
so you came back yet again
then it started in Boystown,
Christopher Street, the Gayborhood
you was 14
when mama n daddy cudn't have you corruptin' the
otha' chirren' with that homosexual spirit
so you struck it alone
in a world where being black is a death sentence
being black and trans turn you into a zombie
cuz' even in death your body seem to haunt them
they found you
one limb on 34th
and the other in a dumpster on 63rd
after a trick had let you baptize them in the waters of your divinity
but turned violent when the tides took them
into a place they'd neva' seen
but you refusing to let go of a life you had
finally found the courage to live
reassembled yourself
not like a vase put back together with nostalgia and gorrilla glue
but a Phoenix
rising from the dawn to greet a day you were promised
for you have survived holocausts since inception
so what's a belch to a tornado
what's a forest-fire to a supernova
and what is death, to a muthafuckin' Phoenix
when resurrection, is your morning yawn
you arise each day after they kill your spirit, hopes, and sanity
and still manage to find enough of it to keep moving on
you have survived trips across the ocean in ships
that you should never have known
whips dancing on your back fasta' than Step N' Fetchet combined
and dodged bullets like the rain

and now
here you are
standing in front of the world
daring it to bring on the next apocalypse
because when the bombs make
impact and the smoke clears
there you will be
black, trans, and still breathing

Puzzle Box
Rahne Alexander

The love of my life received a Rubik's Cube at Christmas. She pulled it out of the package, and everyone around the room had a story to share as they passed it hand to hand.

Someone would make a twist and then twist it back saying, "Oh, well we don't want to get it all messed up on its first day!" and then pass it to the next person, who silently repeated the ritual.

The Cube landed in my hands for a minute and I rolled it between my fingers, feeling the familiar creaky framework shift slightly with each roll. It had been twenty years and change since I last solved one of these. Time was you could drop any Cube in my hands in any condition and thirty seconds later it would be restored to its pristine state. "I used to solve these so fast," I said. Someone else in the room did too.

I was there for the first wave of the popular puzzle. Of course, I wanted one, but we were poor and that meant waiting for knockoffs. I accepted my condition. My first Cube was a keychain-sized version, complete with a grommet jutting out of one corner. The cheap structure threatened to collapse at any moment. I worked with it anyway; it's what I had and it functioned more or less like it should.

A full-sized Cube arrived in my hands soon enough, as did a slim paperback promising to teach me *How To Solve The Cube In Less Than A Minute*. In my haughty youth, I scoffed at the sloppy grammar of the book title. It would take me more than a minute to read and absorb the Book.

Before the Book, I had not solved the Cube on my own. My preferred puzzles are language-based. Spatial puzzles can be fun distractions, but I tire of them easily.

Still, I held hope that with time I might stumble across a solution of my own for this Cube, based on the hints from the Book's prefaces... but no dice. The Book's instructions were the only thing to give me the surefire pathway to perfection.

Slowly I began adopting the Book's methods: Pick a side and perfect its face. Ensure that the first ring around the sides was complete and move to Stage Two, completing the belt around the center. Then Stage Three, the bottom ring and face—the most complicated stage—as every move down below would displace something above.

The Book contained simple illustrations and detailed, precisely-coded instructions for every possible scenario. I was irritated by the coding. I felt it was inelegant. There had to be scenarios in which the Book would be useless to me, to anyone—like when a Cube had been reassembled incorrectly, or when a Cube had its stickers swapped. *Surely this ugly little Book had overlooked a few possibilities.*

The Stage Three directions were the most precise. If your corner piece needed to be turned one hundred twenty degrees to be properly positioned, here's what you do. If your corner piece needed to be turned one hundred twenty degrees and moved to the opposite side, this is how you get there without losing all your progress.

I studied the moves and rehearsed them, growing rapidly more adept. My fingers became more nimble when holding the Cube. I'd get to Stage Three in a matter of seconds and then begin turning the cube lightly under my finger pads to analyze the positions to complete the Cube. Before long, I could replicate the moves rapidly and bring the Cube to equilibrium in a minute or so. I wasn't terribly motivated to make record time; the world record holder basically looked at a Cube and it was solved. It was enough for me to solve a Cube so that I could then begin making patterned variations of the Cube's perfect state, with five spots on all faces being my favorite.

Eventually, and without fanfare, I put away the Cube. Twenty years and more rolled away, and I found myself holding a brand new Cube, feeling the familiar weight. "I used to solve these so fast," I said. Someone else in the room did too. I handed it to her and moved on with the holiday festivities. By the end of the day, the Cube's colors were fully mixed.

That evening I restored a top face—not a difficult task for most—and began spinning the Cube lightly by the corners. There, an unexpected muscle memory rushed back to me. I started twisting and found that I'd completed the second band without a thought. It was shocking how fast this had come to me.

Stage Three, however, did not return to me so easily. I'd give it a go, but the autopilot that brought me to the brink just wouldn't engage. I'd set down the Cube for a bit and then come back to it a few days later, scrambling everything and starting again, hoping that momentum would push me through to the end. Slowing the motions didn't help me to understand them. Every time, I'd slam into my Stage Three roadblock.

My beloved would say, "I'm sure you could look it up," and I'd agree. But that wasn't the point. The point was less for me to re-learn the path to perfection and completion, but instead for that knowledge I'd absorbed as a child to seep to the surface.

This went on for almost a year. But then one evening, I twiddled and twaddled and suddenly the Cube was restored. It was a mystery how I arrived at this version of perfection, but I had to take it. I hadn't been tracking my moves, but there it was, plain as day, solid on all sides, just as Rubik intended.

I immediately began making the patterns I preferred. Those moves came back with remarkable ease as well. I began using the Cube as a guitar pick cushion and the year rolled to a close. At the start of the next year, I decided to see how long it might take me to replicate the miracle. As of this writing, fourteen months later, it remains unfinished. Eventually, I'm certain, this puzzle box will arrive at perfection again on my own terms, and then we'll see what happens after that.

Before They Were Flesh

Magpie Leibowitz

The attic of the synagogue is cold in the winter, even as spring approaches with the death and rebirth of the sun. Though the building has long been vacant of a congregation, memories play along the rafters like the smoke that used to rise from the ever-lit lamps when there were still those to light them. Some say the memories, too, are dying—like the moss and mold once thick on the ceiling feeding on the condensation of hushed breaths and the worried gossip and the death of a people.

Today, though, they bloom.

It is almost Hanukkah. The fire of life in oil, smeared on the pavement of eternity, outlives its allotted lifespan, even in self-immolation.

Outside, there is no snow, only rain. It meets the warmth from below in the corners of the attic where the joints in the roofing, however crafty they were a millennium ago, have grown holes. Steam rises from the sloping floor, up to the tiled roof, down to the gargoyles, in storage from the cathedral.

It's been years since the cathedral collapsed. The vaulting caved first, and then the roof fell and the looters came and stole the gilding on the altar and dispersed it like stones cast, like prophecy unfulfilled. You can see the building from the old town, a hulk of stone in the shape of a ribbed torso on its back. In the old town, so unlike the cathedral and the castle beside it, there are still those who remember, who remember even the synagogue, but that memory is unlike the memory of the day the cathedral was looted.

It was an earthquake, some say. Others tell of a new bomb. Something shook the hill and cracked the cathedral into golden, jeweled splinters, fragile and beautiful as a fabergé egg. In some places, a story that holds that memory never dies. Memory has a death grip on the living, and the bombs that fell and were buried and defused never really left the ground. They were only waiting for the right moment to explode.

The gargoyles roll their eyes at this. They leave their tongues out-stretched as though to catch the light from the holes in the roof. A pale imitation of light through stained glass; it leaves their bellies empty.

So long ago, they fired clay from the Vlatava and made the man that now huddles between the gargoyles. They burned him in a furnace, like others burned his people's bodies, though they meant to make him immortal. When his work was done, they left him broken in a room full of bones, like all attics and all basements; bones and people who live on bones and marrow.

Clay, like other bones, is blessed and fertile. In some stories, it was clay from which all life grew. And so they thought they could turn bonemeal and clay into life. And where a soul should be, if such a thing exists, they left a hollow which fills with water through the trepanned holes dripping down from the ceiling.

It's Hanukkah. From the vantage of the attic, it seems the _hanukkiah_ below have lit themselves.

In the heat, a stem protrudes from a clay head. Another wiggles its way from pensive eyes, and another down through an aquiline nose. The body is soft inside, its softness grows, and the roots push their way through the skin.

Spring comes, and the snow on the roof soon drips through the derelict shingles. On shabbat, sometimes, there are rare footsteps that echo through the nave. Careful footsteps and no voices.

Soon, a crow, and then a dove, build their nests sheltered in the brick gable.

Soon, it will be pesach.

The body grows softer. Mud, now; he melts into the plant within who wonders how she'll survive when he's gone? What will she eat, when the people are gone, where there's only crows and doves and the rare footsteps though no bodies for them to belong to?

She knows she'll find a way. She has always found a way. When she was a seed, washed up on the Vlatava, and the Rabbi Loew planted her, unknowing, in the golem, she put herself to sleep. She curled and dried, hidden from the heat, but the heat found her. In the space above candles, before burning, she reached out to the heat and the water and the worms in the ground below.

She didn't reach out to the Rabbi, or the people, because she knew they would die. They died hoping, always. They always died. She remembers the sound of the burials, the taste of the shovels, the smell of dirt, how it felt to be alive in the soil before they dug her up to bury more bodies.

In summer, she tries the ladder down from the *genizah*. The attic has made her afraid and hungry. There are others who always come to attics and basements like these, where there are so many papers to be forgotten in archives. Papers, objects waiting to be buried; this is the *genizah's* purpose, a waiting place for the word between here and the world beyond.

She knows that she, like the papers and the golem, is unusual, meaning interesting. They will try to keep her alive, though all she wants is to dig herself into the ground. She knows that not all burials are for the dead, though she seeks herself in the cemetery.

There will be no headstone for her. No stones to lay on her grave. No one to lay them.

And they will come for papers to burn, papers to eat, anything to survive the long, warming nights.

Others will come. They will come in memory. They will come in myth. Because it was said, the way our prophecies always are, that when deliverance is needed, the golem, like the messiah, will deliver them. Unto whom, though? And when? And when?

And when there are no more papers, no more synagogues, no more people, what will happen to the gravestones and the stones left for them? Who will wonder, silent in the graveyard, what more can anyone offer the dead or the living, but stones?

Canary
Connifer Candlewood

We live and die under a microscope. The drones,
the informant, the algorithm. Our lives are
broken down and digitized and looked at on a graph.
There are no coincidences, there is a stage. A lie.

We are not about to lose our way though the path is non-
binary. We are the canaries in the tunnel transmuting through
earth. We will defy death and strip out the old mold.

We deny that chances can be sold to the highest bidder. We are
bitter, we are strange and we will change for them no more. Kill
your idols, their masters. Become the one that you sought after.

We are not yellow because we are afraid, it is because
we hold the sun within us. With clear eyes and clear
hearts we declare that this is a new day.

Weekend
Casey Plett

Friday before Christmas, I wake up and it's 11:20 AM I'm hungover like usual. I slept through my alarm. I work at a big store in the mall—being late this time of year will be bad. I'd wanted to shower, to make coffee. Neither's happening. My shift starts in forty minutes.

I force up my body, take my meds, chug a Boost, moisturize. I really do move so much slower in the morning without coffee. I don't have time to fix the makeup I slept in. I put on my boots and coat and scarf and head out the door.

It is icy and with five steps outside, I'm on my ass. See, it's not that cold out, it's been just below freezing all week. This is very warm for late December in Winnipeg, Manitoba, where I live, the second coldest city in the world. The dense snowpack melts and re-freezes and melts again, and it makes the ground a big divoted lopsided chunk of ice. Normally we have a deep freeze for months that makes the snowpack-ice-ground smooth.

I get up and go to my car. I do not get in because there is a ridiculous fucking inch-thick coat of ice on my windshield and my window. Usually it's less than a millimeter. I start the car, grab my little sharp plastic scraper and give 'er. It instantly breaks and snaps off in my hand.

I get my older one, the long handle of wood with the brush with the scraper that isn't as sharp. I slowly chip away. The ice is so thick. I'm going to be late. I call the store. No one picks up; it's fucking Christmas.

I drive and realize I've forgotten to bring a new pack of cigarettes. I get to work only ten minutes late. They're not mad.

The day at the store passes ok, breezy and unnotable. It's Christmas, sure, but not unmanageable. I used to work at the Strand in New York during Christmas, I would clock out with a drain in every muscle. It ain't bad here. It's calmer.

A lady calls wanting to exchange a book she bought a year ago. Ha.

I drive home and make a sandwich and load up Duolingo. The sandwich has lots of fibre and is very specifically calorie-calibrated, as is everything else I've eaten today and for the last few weeks.

I decided, some time ago, that I want to be skinny and I want to speak French. I was skinny once, for about a year, and I spoke French once, decently off and on for a few years. I want to be those things again, and for longer.

I pour a drink of alcohol, which is not calorie-calibrated.

My phone goes off, it's one of the girls I drive. I drive sex workers. That's my night job. I was off it for a while, but I've started again. I drove this girl, Tania, last night. It was a short call, to an inn out by Polo.

I eat my sandwich before leaving.

This call is way out on Portage, almost to the west Perimeter. I have to drive east to pick her up then double back. It's a single house and she hasn't seen him before. I'm nervous because I don't have the new number for the agency she works for. Then again, I'm always nervous.

Behind the curtains, the guy's silhouette is barely visible but clearly headed towards the door. I pull forward on the street, park, take out a book.

Ten minutes later, Tania's back in the car. *He was a fucking cunt!* she says to her boss on the phone. *He took the money back out of my hand and I should've punched him in the fucking face. Next person who takes money out of my hand is getting punched in the face.* Turned out dude wanted her to do something which cost more, which he claimed to have cleared with the agency, which he hadn't. And then refused to pay more. And then took the money out of her hand.

This kind of thing happens a lot. Bad calls, bad in the sense that guys refuse to pay, try to get other things, etc. I've driven so many calls like these. Even guys who just get off on fucking with hookers. Who knows.

Tania pays me twenty for the ride as opposed to the usual twenty-five. That's fair.

Two months since I got back from book tour, where I sold dozens of a book I wrote and maybe fell in love, I'm back to this life and working so, so much. I do okay for money really, but working at the store just wasn't going to cut it. So, here we are. Sometimes it's as if those weeks on tour reading in basements and cafes and bars in a new town every night, drinking and laughing with new beautiful faces every night, were a dream. Is life just like this now? Beyond the foreseeable future? Who knows. It's tiring, and sometimes scary. I'm not happy right now. I'm really not happy about my life. But there are good parts to it, and worse things.

I get home and pour another drink and start reading for a freelance assignment. I do this while checking Facebook.

After an hour, I get a text from another girl I drive: Sam. Can I drive after two AM? Will I still be up?

I'm already groggy and it's only midnight, but I could use the money. And I worry about Sam often—she's a young trans girl, kinda new to the scene, and doesn't have the savvy or instinct most of the experienced girls I drive seem to have. Nor the resources to fall back on. She's from a rez an hour away and doesn't have many friendly people in the city.

Yeah, I'll probably still be up, I say. She says she'll text me.

I keep reading and writing and checking. I fade.

Quarter to two. Very ready to go to sleep. I turn the light off and put the phone basically on my ear. There's a great chance the call won't pan out for a number of reasons (he'll cancel, she'll have an incall in the meantime, she'll go to sleep herself, etc.) and I don't want to wait up for nothing. I've done that before. But there's no way I won't hear my phone now. I drift off in a non-waking drunken state, feeling at peace, floating in equilibrium with my body, nerves preserved and fuzzed and at rest.

I wake up at noon. I have three hours before work. I'm pleasantly hungover, and hungry. Very, very hungry, weak-hungry, a mix of overslept and famished and alcohol-recovered that means I can barely lift my head up or get out of bed.

I like feeling like this. I feel detached and pure and clean. I want to be skinny and speak French, that's what I want from my life right now. I want to be skinny. I want to speak French.

Eventually I check my phone. Sam had asked if I could drive around half past two. Out to East Kildonan, where I drove her to a creep last week who licked her all over her body and got between her and her phone while I was calling and texting out back. The guy eventually relented, I think (think?) because her phone was blowing up. *Oh God oh God is she ok was it that fucking creepster again did she take a cab there did she make it back fuck fuc—*

I get up, make coffee, message a new t-girl in town, Bianca. She's got some extra spiro and breast forms. I text Sam: *Hey sorry, I was so sure my phone would wake me up. Also, do you want any hormones or breast forms?* She texts back right away. *No worries,* she says, *the guy came to her place.* And *yeah, that would be great.*

I answer e-mails and coordinate with Bianca about the spiro and breast forms. I was hoping to write more. But I have to get ready for work.

No shower again. I eat some yogurt, make a sandwich, do my makeup, throw on my winter gear, and head out the door. I don't slip on my ass. The ice on the windshield isn't that thick. I bring my cigarettes and have a good smoke on the way. The traffic sucks because it's the Saturday before Christmas. I get to work a few minutes late. It's all fine.

Two days ago when I was on cash, a doctor from Morden—the small, mean town I lived in as a kid that's about an hour and a half away from this city—came up to my register. His boys used to babysit me. He had a stern, unbroken gaze.

Hey, not to be weird, I'd said. *But did you ever live in Morden?*
Yeah.
You remember a doctor named Aganetha Plett, you work with her?
Yeah.
You remember her son?
He does a double-take and scans my body up and down.

Oh! he said. *Well, okay then.* Then: *How's your mom doing?*

2014, for fuck's sakes.

Say hello to your mother.

Say hello to your boys.

He leaves in a hurry. His last name is also Plett. Fucking Mennonites.

I think about that man at work today. I am one person at this cash register and so not at another, driving sex workers. Should I take time off here so I can write more, and make up the rest by driving? Should I try to get a real job? Should I even keep writing? Who fucking knows, man.

Seven o'clock. Lunch break. I go into the mall and get a big coffee and an espresso shot and eat my sandwich. My phone rings—it's a local number I don't recognize.

Hello?

Hey? Casey? Casey?

Yes this is Casey.

Hi! It's Lina.

LINA!!! Hi!!!!

Lina is the first girl I ever drove, the one who put up the ad for "female driver wanted" I answered back in the first place. It's been awhile since I've heard from her. *Are you back driving again?* she asks. *I heard you're back driving again! I was worried about you, I wondered what had happened to you, I'm glad you're okay!!*

It touches me. That someone would worry about me. It does not occur to me she didn't call to see if I was ok because... it doesn't matter. Because I know plenty of people (women, almost always women) who I worry about, wonder about, but wouldn't call or text, yet think about with sporadic frequency enough to put a small dose of hope out in the universe thinking *I hope she's ok.*

I'm not saying I, we, couldn't or shouldn't call or text them. I'm not saying it's not good I haven't checked up on people, or that people don't check up on me. It's just that, sometimes, certain people say they worry about me but they have no idea what my life is like. And many of them are misguided (sometimes sweetly, purely so) about what the bad things in my life might be. I'm saying it means something, this worry, coming from Lina.

Lina says she liked me driving for her. She mentions a former driver being kinda skeezy, and then I'm like *yes, yes, I can, of course, I'm at work right now at the store but I'll... I will be here less in the future.*

I go back to work and finish my shift. I talk with a customer who's a local author. He loves to check the sales records of his book. We sold one last year.

I close the store at eleven and open my phone in the staff coat room. Loni's wondering if I can drive her and, also, facilitate an e-transfer from her regular for a Christmas gift.

I get a McDouble on the way out of the mall because I still have calories left to eat today and it's Christmas goddammit and maybe that'll make a rumble in my stomach and launch a big shit I dunno fuck it bodies are stupid.

I sometimes don't want to drive Loni. She can be unpredictable and flaky and does risky stuff like jib (meth) and doesn't always pay me. A few weeks ago, Loni was in a bad mood, distracted, and didn't give me the buzz code for the big apartment complex she went into. Then her phone died and she didn't come out for hours. I waited and waited till my phone died, then called her friend from a pay phone and begged building security to help me find out where she'd gone. Finally, after three hours, when the choice was either cops or go home, I went home (what could the cops even do). My mood kept growing darker, wondering if she'd been doing jib or fell asleep or forgot about me or whatever.

Then the next morning, I had missed calls from her. Turned out the guy had been huge and drunk, then blocked her from leaving. Eventually he passed out and she escaped, but not before she had gotten more scared than she ever had in her whole life.

Loni is also trans.

I tell her I can drive. I ask her if she's at home. I scrape off my car and pick up my burger.

It turns out I'm just taking her to a friend's. We talk about what we're doing for Christmas. *I really am so excited to have a home-cooked meal*, she says. *I haven't had a home-cooked meal in forever.* She'll go to her family out at the edge of Transcona, that sudden line where the city turns into country. She lives with the girl who I woke up worrying about, Sam. Sam isn't doing anything for Christmas. She doesn't get along with her family.

I tell Loni I'll be back when the transfer goes. I go to drive another call where I'm supposed to pick up Shari, a cis lady, but it turns out to be a goose chase. As this is getting figured, I try accepting the transfer on McDonald's Wi-fi in a parking lot in North Kildonan but I need the answer to a security question.

The question is: "What product/service am I paying you for?" BOOM, my red flag go up at that one. I decide to reject it if the answer had anything to do with sex or Loni's name.

The answer comes: *cantfuckinwait.* LULZ.

I drive back downtown and get on a Tim's Wifi from the parking lot. The transfer completes. I drive to the RBC on Portage and pick up the cash, then drive to Edmonton Street to pick up Loni, give her the money, and take her back home.

Snow is falling now, soft wet flakes, American-style snow, gently drifting down to cover the road. I'm looking forward to getting the fuck out of my car and snuggling into my bed. I have a family thing out in the country the next day too. It'll be fine, just tiring. I have to get food to bring.

Oh, food. My stomach is growling again already, but it's getting to easier to shush that. I want to be skinny and I want to speak French. I want to be skinny. I want to speak French.

We stop at D's on Broadway for cigarettes. We head north and Loni realizes she needs cat food. *Can we stop at the Sev? I'll pay you another five.* I detour over to Ellice and Maryland.

Shit, I'm no stranger to late-night Winnipeg weirdness, but the party bars in New York that aren't this damn crowded at one in the morning. The snarl in the parking lot is like a grade school at eight-fifty-eight AM. I mark some territory and wait in the car, holding Loni's cigarette. A guy walks by and gives me fifty cents for a smoke.

We drive to where Loni's staying on Isabel Street.

Shari and I might need a ride in a hour, she says, *but if you're asleep we'll take a cab.* (Shari has somehow ended up at her house.)

I'll probably be up, I say.

I drive home wanting bed. The snow has covered the street now. Cars have made clear tire marks. It's beautiful. It never gets like that here. The winter here is different than what you see in a postcard. Normal winter here is caked-on ice, it's the moon, it's infinitesimally small snow raging and horizontal and wind. But the snow is gently falling now, as if sliding down from suspended strings. Peaceful, untouched.

In my room, it's 2 AM. I shuck off my bra and tights and pour a glass of Diet Coke.

I usually add alcohol to the glass at this point. But I don't.

I make to, but then I don't.

I don't want it. It does not feel necessary.

I don't remember the last time this happened.

I put ice cubes in the glass of pop and take a long, deep drink and it's delicious and cold. Particular memory synapses fire. I remember teenage days when I drank soda by the gallon, when I was trying so hard to be a boy, before I'd ever discovered alcohol, before any of this, any of this, any of this.

In the car, I was listening to The Hush Sound. The girl who turned me on to The Hush Sound, when I lived in Portland, was one of my oldest friends. She and I don't talk anymore, and haven't for four years. On the surface, it's my fault. Below the surface, it's still my fault, but it's hers too.

The song I had been listening to is called "The Artist." It's an unusual song for The Hush Sound, whose albums were so young and fresh and... innocent. Innocent is the best adjective I have to describe The Hush Sound, except for this song: "The Artist." My old friend and

---

I really loved this song.

I stand in my room, drinking my soda.

Maybe I'll epilate my legs.

The phone rings mid-electropluck. It's Shari. She wants a ride home now.

I put my clothes back on. Loni texts. *More money from e-transfer regular guy* meant for me and her.

Security question this time: *What to do.*

The answer this time, no bullshit: *drink.*

I pick up Shari. I give Loni some cash and plan to hit the ATM on my way back. Then Shari gets an outcall, a long one out by Talbot, and the guy's gonna give her five hundred. I'll drop her off, wait to hear the call's good, then go home and she'll call me when she's done. That's the way she wants to do it.

We drive through an industrial thoroughfare to get to Talbot.

Shit!! she says. *Is that Ryan?!?*

Ryan is her best friend and the boy she's in love with, and the guy who's been avoiding her for weeks. Also: Ryan is trans. He wants to be a woman. *He won't ever because he doesn't think he'd ever be pretty enough,* says Shari. It should go without saying this made my heart achingly heavy. (Also fuck: The boy's young, already pretty, and soft-featured. Give him a year on estrogen and he wouldn't have shit to worry about in that department.)

I tell Shari then I had that fear too once, a long time ago. It kept me from doing a lot of things. Heartfelt how she usually isn't, Shari says Ryan and I should talk. *Yes, yes, anytime.*

We see this guy walk from huge looming buildings over to houses and down a back lane.

I kinda wanna see if it was him. We double back. It's not.

We get to the house and she calls the client. No answer. I pull over, but she says, *let's just go.* I turn around but go slow because, ugh, it's probably fine, he'll probably re-surface in five minutes and we'll just have to turn around and go back.

Driving up Henderson, she gets a text from him: *Nice pictures. I'm going to put them all over the Internet.*

She snorts. *You're welcome dude. They're already all over the Internet.*

We stop at Subway for her dinner.

The guy continues. He'll put her pictures all over Facebook and Instagram! (*Whatever,* she says, *more business for me.*) He says he'll call the cops! (*I've done nothing illegal,* she points out, *you're the one doing illegal shit by asking for me.*) He starts calling her fat. (*You're the one trying to pay for sex,* she says, and then she's done.)

I drive her home. She's already burned fifty bucks on cabs today, I know. She asks me how much I want. I ask for half of my usual rate.

Last word from the guy: *I'm going to tell the cops you live on Henderson!!!* We both laugh. She never gave him the number and Henderson runs half the length of the entire city anyway.

Driving back home, I detour to Shopper's on Osborne and pick up a big bag of chips for the family thing tomorrow and suck out the cash from the e-transfer. I play "The Artist" one more time. I hope I don't give in and eat the chips before I leave tomorrow. I should load up Duolingo before I sleep. I want to be skinny. I want to speak French.

It's December 2014 and I'm twenty-seven years old. I don't know what my life is supposed to be. I don't know what's supposed to come next.

The snow had stopped a while ago and it's no longer new, mulched up and slushy now on the roads. At home, I count my money, put some in a savings envelope, and some in my wallet. I plug in my phone and pour vodka, a lot of vodka, a regular amount of vodka, into the soda that's left in my glass. I eat the entire bag of chips reading news on the Internet. A roommate scrabbles, talking worriedly on the phone about missing something. She goes out the door, her car pulls out, then returns a half hour later. A cat scratches my door. I resolve not to weigh myself for another week. I listen once more to "The Artist." I check Facebook, I write and write, eventually I've written a lot, eventually it's six-thirty AM and I'm fucking hammered. It's still dark outside because it's the solstice now in Winnipeg, Manitoba, the second coldest city in the world. It will be dark for a couple more hours. If I go to bed now, I can get three hours of sleep before getting up to see my family. If I make it back in mid-evening, I can get the spiro and breast forms from Bianca, then drive over and give them to Sam.

1 AM

Ana Valens

You stare at the bathroom mirror and your hairless body stares back at you. You feel like something out of a Dalí painting: surreal, abstract, hard to put into words. Your body is an artistic mess.

Your tiny hips and broad shoulders clash with your puffy tits. Your neck is too muscular to hide your Adam's apple, and your chin is too long to look charming. The only good part of your body is your ass, but even that's too blocky for six-foot-two. And don't even bother mentioning the soft lump of limp flesh under your crotch, where your vagina should be.

What a mess.

You run your hands down your chest. The last thing Mom said before kicking your sorry ass out of the house was that you were a phony. A liar. A pervert. That you'd always be deranged. That you're nothing more than a fake. And somewhere deep inside, you think she's right.

So you look at your body: your naked, shitty body, locked inside the gas station mirror. Somewhere between the third and fifth minute, your mind wanders, and you start wondering when your girlfriend is going to pick you up. You fix your tuck, you take a deep breath, and you consider how long she can keep you at her place, until your pills run out and you both go broke.

MEMORIES.seq

CHRYSALISAMIDST

The story of my life
I'm more than eager
To speak

On how my days bleed together
An endless existence of worry, dread, and longing
To be put out of my miseries.

As I turn the looking glass back on myself
I see people drowning in my eyes

Lost in the forests of my hair.

A fantastical world alien to me.
Rendered in real pain. Real trauma.
You refuse to see.

Mosca's Last Ride
Sascha Hamilton

Danny Lee and I walk the ballast at the edge of town at night. The only sound around us are our hushed voices and feet crunching on the rocks below. I feel my heart pounding relentlessly, as it has for weeks now. Depression has its claws in my heart, all summer long. We make our way west out by Emma Road, where this city gives way to old houses and older streets.

This is where we came to say goodbye to you so many years ago. Mourning drag, funeral parade and all. Watching your raft sink to the bottom of the French Broad and holding one another in the setting sun.

I'm getting ahead of myself though. My body holds onto these memories, these stories. Danny says, "You gotta write this all down, it's important," and he's right. In the end, nobody will tell your story but you. This is part of our story, our secret history. Every one of us is a hero, villain, fool, and occasional failure; we are all tied up in our awkward bodies.

I know tragically little about where your story started, though others would fill me in on some of the details later. But I remember exactly where our pages first turned to the same chapter. 2003. Hannah and I thunder down Lipan Street. Skateboard wheels on pavement. It's the sound I am as accustomed to as much as my mother's voice. I am twenty-two years old, entering adulthood, and I wake every morning with the feeling that the world is burning. Always burning, and I move through it on borrowed time. We wake on dirty floors to an endless war. I can't help but feel it's all coming down around us. Twenty-two years old. All of my friends all around. At the show, the bar, the secret spot. Sometimes amidst the laughter and sounds of bottles clinking, I stop and listen. This city, it's an engine. You can hear it grinding down, grinding on. Grinding over. Progressing against itself. I stay out at night, walking, riding, listening. Engine pulse. When it quiets down to a hum, then I feel at peace.

You are in the front yard. I see you for the first time amongst the dry, West Denver desert grass and debris. That image of you is burned into my head forever. Dirty green dress, grandma grasses, five o'clock shadow, hands and face covered in tattoos. Wild eyed and smiling like a maniac. Your dog at your side.

I can still see your aura, if you believe in that shit. Part madness, part wounded, a little fearless, and almost entirely irreconcilably criminal.

We make small talk. I don't remember what about. Hannah and I have to leave. I push off on my skateboard. Your pit bull lunges and latches on, pulls it out from under me, and begins to run away with it in her mouth as if it is a bone. I am sure she is going to snap my skateboard in half, then maybe go for my leg.

"CHESSIE BORDEAUX, YOU DROP THAT SKATEBOARD RIGHT NOW!"

I liked you both from the start.

Winter comes long and cold like so many before. This half-freezing house on the west side of downtown may provide shelter, but offers no sanctuary—not from ourselves and not always from the world outside. If its walls could talk, what stories would they tell? The lives we could have, maybe should have, led? The victory songs we fear to never sing? The steps and missteps, tragedy and triumph. Some nights I think I want to die, but really I think I just hate being alive in a world that forgot how to be gentle. I can't stop crying. I pace my room, I scream, I claw at my face and hair. When they say we will be at war forever, one way or another, that's exactly what we get, even if it looks like angry red slashes crisscrossing my arms or my friends drinking themselves to hell and back every night.

There is a cold night in February. Our friend is in the hospital. My vision goes red, my stomach fills with ice, and there are some things you can never forgive. I sit in the alley, eyes red, crying angry tears. Throwing bottle after bottle into the dark, listening to them smash. Leaning into Jess's shoulder, wishing for solace or meaning in the world. Come three o'clock in the morning, I stomp up the stairs to my room, but sleep is a long time coming.

That tape of the Vengeance LP plays over and over that night. Distorted sounds as ugly and vicious as I feel on the inside.

I pace around this room: blue walls, adorned with photos, cold air, grey floor. There is a photo of Sarah and I on the 101 North, "I love life, I love you" scrawled below it. I run my hand across the picture sometimes when I walk to bed at night, touching the memory, finding comfort where I can. The nights are long.

Spring comes, persuasive as ever. You roll through, and we jump in the van headed east. Denver to Kansas, Kansas to Oklahoma, Oklahoma to Texas. It's hot and dry. I lay in the back of the van rubbing Chessie's belly and listening to your stories. We get pulled over once, and I sit in awe in the back of the van as you convince a befuddled state trooper that you are actually your older brother, using nothing but a previous speeding ticket as your identification.

Austin, Texas. I've never been here before. Ten years older, you show us around the streets you called home in your youth. That particular warzone known as punk in the 80's. Life on the streets and off them. The time heavy metal kids shot your principal and the military recruiter in your high school. The time Pamela Anderson gave you a hundred dollars. (I still tell that story sometimes. Sometimes people don't believe it, but it's too weird to not be true.)

I hold onto it all in my jaded mind, in my body. Chronicling the lost. Our secret history.

In the sticky hot Austin night, we stay at an ancient punk house; it has been here since the late 80's. Kylee and I sleep in the abandoned house next door. You poke your head in the window sometimes, bringing us coffee or candles. Sometimes you send Chessie to wake us up in the morning, happily licking our sleepy faces and wagging her tail. We lay there at night, listening to the city, writing, or kissing. This isn't the life I want to live forever, a moldy house at the edge of town and struggling to feel anything, but it will do for now.

A decade later, some of the details are hazy. There were front porch stories, lots of walks, and a punk show that looked like something straight out of one of the *Mad Max* movies.

A week after, you dropped us off on the highway outside of town. You gave Kylee a knife, wished us luck, and we watched you drive away. We caught rides to Arkansas, then North Carolina. I never saw you again, just like that. Life is fleeting, beautiful, and tragic like that. We were never close, sure. But you were my friend, and I looked up to you.

I called to say I wanted to visit, twice, and you offered to open your home to me, twice. I ended up stuck on the highway outside of Richmond. Twice. You never told me trying to hitch with a dog was so hard.

Then of course, I finally did make it to see you, for the last time, to say goodbye. The call came on Saturday morning.

I looked at my phone. There were three missed calls in under five minutes. Never a good sign. Did I ever tell you? I was walking patients into the abortion clinic, past all these disgusting men, mutilated fetus pictures, and endless bible quotes.

The voice on the other end of the line was shaking. "She died last night." I hung up my phone, kept my head down, and jumped on my bike to ride home. To this day, I consider it a small victory that I didn't lose it in front of the protestors. You know how those motherfuckers are—preying on any emotion—and I would have punched one of them, then and there. I rode home as fast as I could and laid in bed with Hope, crying.

The next day, or the day after, we drove all night through the wind and rain to say goodbye. It's hurricane season in the south, and we got the tail end of one as it dissipated on its way inland.

The day was grey and muddy. I walked up the stairs into your house. Chessie was curled up on Josh's bed all alone. I sat down next to her. Realizing I had never seen one of you without the other, it hits me like a storm: *you are gone forever.*

Mourning drag, funeral parade, painted faces, and instruments. West on Chestnut, left on Montford, down Haywood. We walk to the river, your funeral barge in tow, the band playing your songs.

At the river, the raft is laid out. We draw on it, write you letters, tell stories. We sing to you. I close my eyes and try to find the strength to believe you can somehow still feel how beloved you were. The sun starts to hang low in the west. Your raft is set alight and sent down the river.

Of course, being made by punks, it sinks almost instantly.

We hear the whistle before we see it. Long and loud, getting closer. I feel the ground rumble, the train rolls through, slow and steady. Some of us cry, some of us laugh, most of us just do both. You loved trains so much; of course, you caught that westbound just in time to take you safely home.

That was the day I stopped believing in coincidences.

Later, they would tell me that a train blew past your funeral procession in Kentucky too. Josh swore that your coffin was lighter after it passed.

"I think she caught it," he said.

Three years later, Asheville is my home, and I live in your room. The place I never got to visit you; the place where you left this world. Sometimes when it's quiet, I say goodnight to you before I go to sleep. Sometimes, I ask what you think of the outfit I am trying to wear. So many times, when my body dysphoria gets the better of me, when I feel like my skeleton wants to crawl out of my skin and never come back, I ask you questions and try my best to hear your answers. I have so many questions on nights like this, when my skin just doesn't fit. I know you knew what that was like. You wore it so bravely, long before I did, this awkward, beautiful, mismatched, survivor skin.

Three years. We are getting the baby I nanny ready to go out. She isn't even a year old yet. She sits at the edge of my bed, playing with her favorite stuffed animal that lives in my room. Still so young and her life already tumultuous and unsteady, like so many other children. Her back is to us. A breeze blows through the room, even though the windows had been left closed. She looks up and into the corner of the room. *Oh Mosca, did you see that baby's smile? Did you hear how she laughed? How she clapped and waved?* We can't see you, but I know that was you. Who else could it be? This is your room after all. For a second, I close my eyes and, not fooled by sight, I see you.

I saw you in that child's smile and delighted eyes, and I knew in an instant you were safe, hale, and whole. Beyond the veil. In that warm place beyond hate, hurt, and bitter cynicism. Where I long to see you again one day, through kind eyes, like that child's. When the last curtain falls. When we can let free our masks and finally feel at ease in our own skin.

Three years after that, I said goodbye to Chessie: the first pit bull I ever loved. I can still see the way you two looked, how you fit when you walked together, and I can see it now: safe and beyond all harm.

Thank you for making the baby laugh.

Thank you for teaching me the lesson of being brave enough to ask for help when you need it the most.

Holy Love
Talia C. Johnson

Who are we when our holy love is pathologized?
When we are told that our very identity is wrong
That we are sexual predators
That we are pedophiles
That we are gay men
That it is only autogynephilia
That it is based on a desire to fetishize our own genitalia
That we are intrinsically disordered
That it is something to be cured, done away with

Who are we when our holy love is reduced to our genitals?
When we are told that they only exist to trap straight men?
When TERFS and conservatives tell us that the
genitals we were born with define us
That we have always been men
That we are still men
That we will always be men
That we mutilate ourselves
That we deceive ourselves in thinking we are women
That we must accept what God gave us when we were born

Who are we when our holy love is a source of pain?
When our sexual organs are not those that
our identity and soul require
When our genitals are seen as that of men
When we can barely touch our genitals
When we can barely look at ourselves in the mirror
When our voice is a deep bass
When having to shave our face causes pain
When we cannot bear others touching our body
When our bodies will never be feminine enough

Who are we when our holy love is content with our body?
When our factory issued genitals are not a source of discomfort
When they can be touched as part of our holy love
When we do not want to change them
When they are a source of pleasure
When we are more than our genitals
When we love our voice and embrace its depths
When our bodies are feminine enough
When our whole body is a source of pleasure

Who are we when our holy love is told it cannot embrace the divine?
When we are told we are abominations in the sight of God
When we are told that we must be men
When we are told that we must pray away the trans
When we are told we are not welcome in synagogues
When we are told we are not welcome in mosques
When we are told we are not welcome in churches
When we are told we cannot be leaders in our faith tradition
When we are told our transitions cannot be celebrated

Who are we when we embrace holy love in our body?
We are full human beings, able to be in the world
We are more than our genitals and they do not define us
We are defiant of those who would demonize
us for our genitals at birth
We are at peace with our bodies and their configuration
We are able to engage in physical manifestations of love
We are sexy, we are sensual, we make love with our bodies
We celebrate our bodies and their wonderful diversity
We are able to look in the mirror and hear our own voices

Who are we when we embrace holy love in our spirit?
We are connected with who we are, embracing ourselves
We are reflections of the divine that is part of each person
We celebrate our transitions and identities
in our spiritual communities
We are in relationships that nourish us and those around us
We are at peace with our identities, able to be who we are
We are nourished by the holy love we have for ourselves
We are healers of the world, bringing healing to others
We are lovers in every sense of the word.

May There be Peace in Our Time

AR Mannylee Rushet

?
I wonder what it means

Cause what does peace mean to negro?
I study this shit and *nowhere* is peace found.
If there is peace to be found, it is in companionship and family.

This family is structured in many ways: it is
the roots of the tree you grow out of,
it is the pot you've been replanted in,
and it is roots ripped out of soil.
Still you find a way to survive.
Amongst all the plants who will inevitably do the same,
What. Is. Love. Then.; What. Is. Love. Now;
What. Does. Love. Mean?

I have no way of reasoning this,
which is what I do with everything.
I try to reason them into submission—

the thoughts in my head—
at least until we come to an understanding.
We almost never do;

we just sit there panting after
and chasing each other
back and forth.
Fine,
one of us will say to the other.

Go watch your fucking porn.
Be miserably happy again!

Did I ever know what it was?
Watching reruns of the Disney Channel?
Little Bear, Rugrats, Clarissa Explains It All?
The Amanda Show, Drake & Josh, All That?
Degrassi?

That childhood wasn't love.
Memories made by people
making false ones.
Memories that look good in picket-fence picture frame,

of a time
when you didn't need porn to jerk off;
your imagination of the feeling was good enough.

When was the first you knew you were gay/bi/queer?
Not that building up to knowing feeling,
but when you knew.
Was it 16? Would it zigzag and finally erupt at age 24?
Becoming clear as a dance to you in
brother's/sister-in-law's/your room.

These are some of the clearest
memories of childhood I own.
Sometimes I hope the rest aren't me
being too harsh on myself/others.
Sometimes mental illness leaves me
wondering if I'm feeling things that aren't there.

Do they like me,
or am I making this up because it's the
easiest thing I can get my hands on?
Am I right, or am I just in need of validation?

To map a femme you must open them but
to protect themselves they must stay closed.

Pulling against wind to slam their doors.

Remember, lines between femme and masc are never straight;
they are trap doors.

What does peace mean when there's always war?
What does it mean when there always has been war?
What does it mean to love when it is endless?

Wednesday Morning, 7:26 a.m.

erica, inchoate

Morning.
Morning!
What'll ya have?
Double tall soy mocha, no whip.
Anything to eat?
(*squints at pastry case, decides against starch*)
No thanks.
It's Erica, right?
Yeah.
4.05, please.
Here's five-oh-five.
And a dollar back, be up in a second, have a good
Wednesday.

And I wait.
And I wait.

The white, "radical," rail-thin trans woman making my drink points her usual death stare at me. I don't know her name, but she definitely has the multiple pieces of flair about her pronouns on her jean vest. Occasionally, I see her on the bus when I'm going over to my friend's place. She spends the entire time staring at me. If staring could catch a human on fire, I would be a story in the local alt-weekly about the girl who burst into flames on the 44.

And I wait.
Aaaaaaaaaaand I waiiiiiit.
People who placed their order three minutes after me get their coffee. It's part of the passive-aggressiveness. She waits for a white guy to be waiting before she outs me to him.

ERIC!

Mind, there's an A after it on the cup. Eric is not my dead name; never has been. It's pathetic, but this is what passes for discourse in the world of white trans women these days when you live in River City, where all trans community is white trans community.

ERIC!

The white man looks confused, but gamely corrects her when he notices that it says Erica.

The double tall soy mocha is shoved in my direction with a spiteful growl. I don't think I saw her spit in it...

Why does this keep happening?
Am I supposed to be wearing a button?
Am I supposed to look different than I do?
Am I supposed to be thinner?
Am I supposed to be whiter?
What *am* I supposed to do?

I like your coffee. I am somewhat dependent on a consistent dose of coffee, much like I am somewhat dependent on a consistent dose of estrogen and...alright, let's face it, I am really dependent on a consistent dose of coffee. It's the cheap ADHD medication that you don't get your doctor in trouble with the State for taking.

This means I'm somewhat at the mercy of coffee-slingers, or alternately the tragic coffeepot in my fourteenth floor perch here in River City. I could tell you tales of the thing, but I've descaled it. I live here in reality where I can't be out at work, and where I don't live in the gayborhood, so I'm forty-five minutes away from whatever is allegedly happening. The gayborhood, by the by, is built over the ruins of Black culture in this town that the garrote of gentrification killed slowly, brutally, and intentionally. The idea of trans community churns out of reach; I could get the same experience Coffee Lady gives me at the support group and the local trans women's group on le faceyspace that is only for in-group "cuties."

You know what else reminds you you're the Other? The death glare. The ever-so-clever "Eric." The idea that a trans woman's worth reflects solely on if she's a size six or not. The idea that being fat or disabled or not white or not "girly enough" or me, a combination of all of those things, somehow invalidates my gender or the expectation that others treat me with dignity. I'm fairly certain "he" and "Eric" does not respect either my gender or my dignity.

I'm also fairly certain that there's some sort of imagined competition going on there. One thing I've gleaned about the white trans woman is the weird, cutthroat competitiveness. The idea that you have to compete at femininity, at being Woman Enough. I hate it because, really, you're probably enough, or even Enough. The idea that "Woman Enough" should be enforced by other trans women is outdated, backstabbing bullshit.

The same competitiveness is often extended to the strangest things. It's not okay to post about hockey, but it's somehow cool to spin meaningless praxis into bullying? Or the shoving and pushing that happens when the white folks cast the net for a Good Little Token? Y'all smirkingly take that and call it "sisterhood."

I have sisters, chosen and familially-assigned, and in one case even biological. I have goddaughters and cousins and a stray nibling or twenty. Some of them are trans; most of them are not. Some of them are also intersex; almost all of them are not. But they're my family. They lift me up and they remind me about what I wanted to be before my dreams went up in smoke.

And another thing: none of those family members call me a man. That, you see, is what makes trying to sail my little boat in white-led, white-centered trans community so strange. What things can you go to alone without meeting social sanction? If this says "cuties and friends of cuties," do I have to bring a conventionally attractive white person? When an event is limited to "femme of center" trans women, am I going to be "femme enough?" Will it be inclusive of all disabled people and not just the ones who have invisible disabilities that never discuss their needs with you so they can be "abled enough" to fit in?

Evolution is part of the resilient spirit, and evolution is the only way we can stop being so gosh darn predictable and change the rhetoric about what is acceptable within the trans community. If you want me to be your sister, you need to earn it. You need to show that I won't be disposable when you need to get rid of some pesky token and replace it with a shinier one with a degree from a better college. You need to show that when "colorblind" actors are both kinda ableist and kinda full of it, that you can throw down. You have to protect your people like you protect the Town.

But you have to let us be your people first.

You have to let us into your Facebook groups. You have to stop blocking Brown and Black trans women for being slightly "problematic" instead of giving the admitted and unapologetic rapist her fifth chance. You have to stop using us as props and background noise, an "inclusion" that makes you feel better about yourselves, instead of doing the real work you need to do. And you really, really, really have to stop it with this Day of Remembrance nonsense: a day where a wyt woman moves the goalposts every few years about who counts but refuses to acknowledge anything about race on TDOR's 'official' website.

You have to understand that not everyone grew up with a wyt nuclear family in the suburbs, and you have to quit enforcing those suburban norms in your daily life. The monocultural nature of the white trans community gives the people who work to kill us (like MRAs and TERFs) an opening. It creates a trans community where people actually buy that the indulgence of retweeting a couple of Black community leaders means you're an authority on race. It means a trans community where no trans woman of color can really belong without being white-adjacent (whose wyt allies will eventually turn on as soon as she does something "problematic"). If you expect us to carry water for you constantly, you have to let us in. I don't want to be your goddamn slave.

Or you can keep doing what you're doing right now, but it'd be super great if you could own that you hate Black folk, hate Brown folk, hate disabled people, and really wish fat women didn't exist. Because you'd never be caught dead saying any of this in public, but your actions, as they say, speak louder than words.

Even the word "Eric."

Wednesday morning, 7:32am, a week later

I pause at the point of deciding between Twee Local Coffee Place That Costs Too Much And Can't Find Its Ass But It Sure Has Nice Furniture and Other Not Local Coffee Chain That Won't Serve Me Mermaid Piss But They Use Such Creamy Soy. I am, for one of the first times in my life, actually experiencing what is often misnomered as a "first world problem." Coffee unites the world, really. I have to decide. When I have to decide, I digress, stalling for time, hoping another minute will make it all clear...or that I'll get hit by a comet. Your call.

And I wait.

I go back into the Maw of Misgendering, because I want my bump.

I'd like to tell you it went differently. It did not. The trouble with being a fearful optimist is that sometimes you get your hopes up that today is a new day. And while it's great when it is, it usually isn't. The misgendering and the construction of yet another incorrect dead name? It's supposed to break you, to remind you of your place.

But I'll be back next Wednesday. And my name is Erica, goddammit.

Disabled
Ariel Howland

My natural pace is leisurely and deliberate.
Not fast enough for first grade art.
School taught me I'm too slow to be creative.
I think it was an early sign of autism.

They put me in special ed because I didn't like to read.
The teacher dispensed a pound of Splenda
in every sentence.
How condescending does an adult have to talk
for a six-year-old to notice?

My parents figured out I had a vision issue,
so I wore an eye patch for a year and heard,
What's that patch on your eye?
What's that patch on your eye?
What's that patch on your eye?
In fourth grade, I was told I read like an eighth grader.

Kids asked if every boy with glasses was my brother.
Bullies called me four-eyes.
Would break my glasses, they said.
In middle school, I wore sweatpants every day.
They felt good for sensory reasons.
Autistic people tend to put comfort over fashion.
Bullies put a stop to that.

In high school and college, I had eczema bad.
I often felt ugly and disgusting.
I still do sometimes.
Once a random man asked me
What's all that shit on your face?

I itched all the time.

I chuckled at worry about poison ivy, rashes, and scabies.
People told me to stop scratching, like that was going to help.
Sometimes they would even grab my arms to stop it.
Transitioning made my skin clearer.

I used to tease guy friends with skin problems,
just take estrogen!

I usually have damaged skin on my hands still.
Adults ask me,
What happened to your hands?
What happened to your hands?
What happened to your hands?

Liquid hand soap stings and hurts.
Especially the industrial pink crap.
Showers used to be worse.
I still feel weird about showering.
I don't usually tell people that.

These are a few moments.
There is so much more.
This poem isn't done.
It's not over.
Ableism isn't over.

I used to think there was something wrong with me.
Now I know there is something wrong with me
and it's called autism!
I'm only half joking.
I look forward to a time when autism doesn't
feel like something wrong,
weighing on my chest.
Internalized ableism is a fucking asshole.

Fuck you ableism.

Burdens
Oti Onum

When I was born, I didn't realize the life I was burdened to live. I didn't understand the responsibilities I would need to be equipped for. I didn't realize I was miracle. I didn't see a spark or an angel. I didn't gaze at the stars, for they weren't visible beyond the cloak of polluted air in the sky. I don't remember the Sun illuminating a path for me clear and refined, no Moon to make wishes to. I recall the silence, the hushed sounds of my mother refusing to cry. Praying in church. Resisting the urge. That sound you get in the back of your throat in the agony you know everyone around you doesn't Comprehend.

I used to sleep in the trunk of my mother's station wagon right after I was out of summer school. She would arrive hours late into the night, and I would sleep until my intuition told me to Wake Up & Go In (smiling). And lo and behold, she would show up dancing down the sidewalk.

As if she heard the ECHO of my wish.

I am the sixth of seven children. Before me, my mother is the second of seven, and before her, my grandmother is the youngest of seven. All poor, all impoverished, all descendants of slaves, and all affected by the legacy of racial trauma—the legacy of neglectful abandonment by family, community, and government.

At the start of my sixth grade year, my family lived behind a hardware store. Every morning, I would wake up to breaths of ammonia and other dangerous chemicals from next door. It was packaged in presentable plastics for people to build and rebuild their houses or refurbish their interior decorations. I'd wake up, wash the next day's laundry in the bathroom sink, put on my uniform, and walk a mile and a half to get to school.

Always late, never early, walk in through the front door. Always the same security guard, always with something sarcastic to say to me. After walking through the front door, I would place my bag on the table next to the school metal detector. I'd walk through and hold my hands out for the next security guard to fan the metal scanner across my body back, then front. I'd wait for them to look through all of my belongings and then shoo their hand for me to rush to class. This was my daily routine for the two years my family lived in that house.

After that, I lived in a car with me, my mother, and my younger sister. Early in the morning, and one by one, we would wash our bodies in the bathroom sink of the gas station. Those days were a lot more difficult. I've never had a room to myself. I've never had the space to think and process things in my life. I've never had the support and acknowledgment from a large body of people. I've never had consistency is my point. This is what makes the Homeless Youth Community in Portland different. I am now able to be proactive in community engagement and volunteer work near my new home. I now feel included and, in so many ways, content.

I say this because I am grateful. I am grateful for New Avenues and its partners taking part in the advancement of ending homelessness. The work that you all do is never dismissed in the minds of those you inspire and are motivated to help. We see you, we appreciate you, and we are grateful, even though we do not know how to express it at times. I want to address you all for your work, even if you feel that it is unrecognized, and someday I will be doing that same work in my community. If I've never said it, I will express it again...

Thank You, Thank YOU, THANK YOU!

To compel change, you become it.

I used to believe courage was about facing danger, but I realized real courage is about facing yourself.

The Most Important Trans Woman I Never Knew

Lilith Dawn

The year I was born, people were singing the new hit song "Lola" by the Kinks. That was the most positive trans representation I would find until adulthood.

Two years prior, Gore Vidal wrote a critically acclaimed novel called *Myra Breckinridge* that was inevitably turned into a critically panned movie. Both the book and its film helped solidify the public's idea that trans women were deceptive rapists of men.

Growing up in the 1970s, I was absolutely unaware of any struggle for trans rights. Hell, I was only dimly aware that trans people even existed at all. *How could I be otherwise?* Trans people were busy being shunned in every conceivable manner: exiled from queer and women's spaces, legislated against, and reduced in the media to both farce and threat at the same time.

I couldn't turn on a television without seeing, time and again, counterexample after counterexample. On ABC's *Soap*, Billy Crystal played a gay character who spent the first two episodes pretending to be trans so he could get SRS and marry his boyfriend who, predictably, dumps him. Trans women are in actuality gay men? *Check!* On *Bosom Buddies*, you had Tom Hanks and Peter Scolari crossdressing solely to live in a low-rent, women-only apartment complex. Gaining access to women's spaces with unfettered male privilege? *Check!* (And bonus points for using Billy Joel's "My Life" to razz anyone who might object to the premise.) Another time I watched a Gallagher comedy special, he was telling a bad joke about the recently transitioned tennis pro Renee Richards playing "mixed singles." He couldn't finish the goddamn joke because it was, to him, that funny. The audience thought it was hilarious too. Trans people as confused and pathetic? *Check!*

Those chronic insults took a toll on an identity I hadn't fully grasped or understood. I had a fair amount of toxic masculinity to navigate at home too, but any alternatives were forbidden.

Then I became interested in sex. With that, I dug into my father's closet looking for answers on that one shelf I previously couldn't reach.

At the time, the so-called Sexual Revolution was in a tailspin with AIDS and Reagan-era conservatism rising. But Dad's porn included stuff from just before then, back when the major adult magazines were trying to broaden their appeal. Nearly every fetish and every sexual subculture I know of today I learned about back then.

Inevitably, I stumbled across the trans porn ads and the occasional quarter-page photo. But I didn't see myself reflected back in that porn. I didn't have the words for it, but I could see this porn was made for the male gaze and that trans women were only fetishistic sex objects.

Then there was this one story, a letter to the editor, in some issue of Club Magazine. It was a long letter, and it could have been an article in its own right. It was written by a swinging, bisexual trans woman sharing one of her more memorable nights. Realizing I could well be biased, I recall it being remarkably authentic.

Up to this point, I only saw trans women having sex with cis men. That's all I knew. I presumed that's the way it was, the way it had to be. But there I was, with proof to the contrary: *trans women could be bisexual too.*

I knew well that I was attracted to women, not men. Knowing that being trans was no barrier to who I could love, new possibilities began to reveal themselves to me.

And with that, I started to experiment with seeing myself as female, mostly when my parents were gone for hours and I could have the house to myself. That lasted for two years, until my father went to fetch the guitar I had borrowed from him and found my stash of women's clothes.

My father, like me, is a passionate person. But he was mired in that very toxic masculinity I mentioned earlier, and that passion turned to abuse easily.

He was calm when he set me aside and told me I had to stop wearing women's clothes. *That scared me.* I wasn't used to him being calm. His need to use restraint when he hadn't before left a deep and terrifying impression on me.

So I pretended I wasn't trans for most of a decade. Maybe my dad bought the routine, but judging from the slurs I got from classmates, nobody else did.

My first year of college away from my home town helped, but so did weight training and eventually growing a beard and mustache. I detested it all and hated myself, but I struggled to articulate why. Denial is powerful.

But so is information.

My father got a blue collar job at a rich kid's college and he pressured me to transfer and move back home. I eventually gave in and came to regret the decision. But there was one boon that saved my life: I got access to the university's computer system and with it, the Internet.

I found IRC and started talking to people, online, in real time. There weren't a lot of us, but what an interesting bunch we all were!

And then I noticed the #crossdress channel.

I didn't have a PC with a modem yet. Most people didn't. I had to use the university labs to access #crossdress. This meant anyone could look over my shoulder and see what I was doing.

It took a week for me to take the plunge.

And a week after that, I had gone to my first trans support group meeting and had a trans girlfriend. Weeks later, the toxic mask of beard and mustache came off and my stash of women's clothing began anew.

Dad found out again.

But by this time, I knew about Marsha P. Johnson, Sylvia Rivera, Sandy Stone, Nancy Burkholder, Phyllis Frye, Monica Helms, Monica Roberts, and many more trans women activists. I knew that the Western, cissexist, natural law framework was not the default. I knew that the biology of gender was complex in any species, and that humans were no exception. My last reservations about who I was had begun to fall away. I was ready to defend the woman I found in the process.

My father was clearly upset over my choice of footwear and my defense thereof. He didn't abuse me though. Instead, he stormed off to bed. And when it came morning, he refused to say so much as hello to me as we went to the university together.

On the ride home, he started to talk—only to ask silly questions and make silly demands.

Are you doing this because you feel like a failure as a man?

No, Dad, that's exactly backwards.

You're forbidden from telling anyone else in the family.

Sorry, Dad, you're the last one to find out!

What gave you the right to tell them? he thundered.

They're my family too, Dad.

He grew up poor, I'm going to the rich kid's school he wanted me to attend, and now he's suddenly worried I'd be unhireable if I transition.

You have no idea how many trans women are in my field, Dad. And fuck your expectation that I engage in economic one-upmanship with anyone, especially you.

Eventually I moved to Seattle, got a technical support gig, hung out with fellow trans dykes, and started taking hormones. I kept the Internet access going, and I kept learning and growing as a trans woman.

From time to time, I think about that bisexual trans woman I read about when I was younger. I hope she is still alive, and that one day I can meet her and thank her for that unlikely life-changer.

I can recite so many names. *Marge,* who first invited me to a support group. *Laura,* who affirmed that I could be loved. *Karen,* who taught me much about AMAB trans bodies. *Maxi,* who pushed me to learn and grow amid great resistance. They're all unlikely to be in trans histories other than my own.

But the most important trans woman in this history of mine? I never knew her name.

It's entirely possible she didn't exist and, but for a few moldering copies of some adult magazine in forgotten basements and in my memory, she practically doesn't.

Still, she was real enough to make a difference.

Isn't that enough?

Her Name was Pearl
Sophia Quartz

It was December 1989 when I became obsessed with mermaids. My melancholy, eight-year-old heart found solace in the inherent freedom behind shapeshifting. Every night, I would wrap my legs in blankets and dream of a sparkling lavender tail that swept me to a sea where I was loved in the real way. *Someday, my prince will come*, I whispered while stuffing a pillow into the belly of my oversized pajamas, practicing the kiss of true love in my bathroom mirror at one-thirty in the morning. *Someday, somebody will wake me up from this nightmare.*

Thirty years later, I would finally wake up. But there would be no kiss, no prince, no tail, and no sea to save me. Instead there was you, another little girl with a story not so different from my own. Together, and seemingly by accident, we wound up rescuing each other. Together, in fact, was finally *the answer*.

*   *   *   *   *

Knock. Knock. Knock.
It began with three little knocks on my door. I was always slightly annoyed, but never at you. Worry fueled my overactive mind back then, and everything I couldn't process in the day came alive in the darkness. Night after night, I didn't sleep. It was the only thing I wanted, for the fucking insomnia to stop so I could rest in a moment of peace and quiet.

"Sophie," you asked in the sweetest six-year-old voice, "will you help me get dressed?"

Half-asleep in my nightgown, I stared blankly across the room, barely able to stay conscious for the thirty seconds it took to open my door. Still, I managed. I refused to lock you out, like my own mother did to me so many years ago.

"Yes, love," I always said, reaching my hand out to yours. "I don't want to be with anyone else but you."

Your eyes glowed brighter than the Sun hearing those twelve simple words. Afterwards, you'd cling to my arm feverishly and drag me up the stairs like I was your beloved dolly. I was, and probably still am, your beloved dolly—*your faithful protector.*

"COME ON SOPHIEEEEEEEE."

At the time, I didn't quite understand the significance of what was taking place between us. I was just a giant woman—a giant, queer, unemployed trans woman with unruly, bright cotton candy hair, lost in her late thirties. You were just the overactive, adorable little boy I lived with, the kiddo with a body that wouldn't stop and a mind that kept flying a million miles a second. *I am not going to get attached to him,* I would tell myself. *It's only temporary. It's always only temporary.*

But then suddenly it wasn't. You chose me. You kept choosing me, again and again, for two years straight. And in the end, I suppose, I chose you.

*   *   *   *   *

"Mama—I mean. . . Sophie. I think I'm a girl."

Mama. I never thought I would hear that word, not to describe me anyway. I was physically incapable of producing sperm at that point, let alone an egg. Complicated feelings about gender, on the other hand, had chased me for my entire life. I spent decades breaking down gender, roasting it over an open fire, and then eating it for breakfast. When I transitioned back in 2006, I thought I was done with all this gender nonsense. I was certain I had tossed it away with the rest of my facial hair, empty boxes of Androcur, and twenty tiny vials of estradiol valerate.

It turned out I had no idea what *done* actually meant.

"Tell me more, honey?" I carefully asked, sitting at your eye level while pursing my lips.

"Well. . ." You stammered a little, carrying a pause like your life depended on it. "I'm a boy on the outside, but a girl on the inside."

My heart sank.

I've heard some people describe gender dysphoria as a constant sadness. For me, it was more like the buzzing of two thousand gnats vomiting over a lost stash of decaying bananas. Everywhere I looked, there it was—**GENDER**—in bold, bright letters. Purple and pink polka-dotted Christmas pajamas. Stuffed mermaid dollies with bright red bangs and sparkling blue fins. Long, windswept hair. Scrunchies. Actual friendship. When I was your age, I desperately longed for the ordinary things every other girl had. Meanwhile, I remained stuck on the lost continent of Oz.

If what you were experiencing was even remotely close to what I survived, I didn't want this for you. I never wanted this life for anyone else ever again.

"What can I do to make this better right now?" I asked.

"Just hold me," you said.

You curled into my lap and poured the weight of your heart into my chest. I don't think either of us moved for at least an hour. When you finally fell asleep, I couldn't stop crying. I knew where this road was heading, and none of it was going to be easy—for either of us.

So we tried it. Your Mama, her fiancée, and I became what you called your Crystal Guardians, and we tried it for six months. Of course, that doesn't include the two months it took to get your father on board. He was convinced that this was all our fault, that our collective hatred of cisgender white men had infected the mind of his innocent young boy. But after some careful negotiating, we struck a deal. And oh my god, you soared.

I remember loving dresses like you did, once when I was ten and later when I was twenty-six. There's something comforting about the way a dress can hang past your hips and cut across the knees. First, it's the twirls, but then it's a freedom you've never tasted before. Like you didn't know it could be that good. I loved watching you spin.

I had never seen you happier in your life.

But being a girl was never really about clothes or makeup. For one thing, you weren't just this overactive child anymore. Your language exploded, and you started finding words to explain all the feelings sitting right under your surface. But my favorite part—*our favorite part*—was the magic. Sometimes I could have sworn your invisible fairy wings were growing as you dashed past everyone on the playground. You were no longer moving to get all of your energy out; instead, you were learning how to fly.

*   *   *   *   *

"Sophie. Sophie, IS THAT YOU? Sophie, WHERE ARE YOU?"

I had just walked in the door from a long day away. I was exhausted, but still excited to see you. You arrived twenty minutes beforehand with Mama. I had tried to time it so I wouldn't be out too late. Clearly, it wasn't soon enough.

"Sophie, you weren't home when I got home," you yelled while scurrying around the house. "Why weren't you here to meet me?"

There you were, staring at me from across the hall in your favorite formal gown, which was completely drenched in mud. Dirt lingered across your eyebrows, and your cheeks were still wet from Mama's foiled attempt at cleaning you up. Today, you went to a wedding on the farm of a family friend. You chose to wear the whitest and fanciest outfit in your wardrobe, and then proceeded to play in it as hard as possible.

I kneeled down to your height, gently brushing the wispy hairs covering your bright, hazel eyes. They were welling up with tears.

"I'm so sorry, honey," I replied while taking your left hand. "Next week, I promise to be here when your dad drops you off."

"Every time," you cried. "Every time I come back to Mama's, you need to be here. I need you to always be here when I am, Sophie. I don't feel safe without you."

You started to trace an invisible outline of my hands with your fingers. Carefully, cautiously, you mapped the distance between the tip of my index finger and the bottom of my wrist.

"I promise to always be home when you come home," I spoke while squeezing your tiny hands. "But even when we are apart, I am still with you. And you're always with me. Always."

Your tears started to slow. You couldn't look at me still, not yet, but your eyes were clinging to every word.

"But what if you die?" you asked. "Will I still be with you then?"

"Even when I die," I replied.

"Even if you got shot by machine guns?"

"Even then." I placed my hand on my heart. "You're still right here."

You slipped away to your room that was conveniently nearby, but only for what felt like a split second. When you reappeared, both of your small hands quickly grabbed ahold of my right index finger and tied a short, white string around the bend until a baby knot appeared.

"This is for when we are separated, so you'll never forget me."

You took the one remaining purple claw clip in your hair and clipped it onto the string, then wrapped yourself around my leg. I couldn't move at all. In the light of that hallway, the clip glistened like a beautiful amethyst stone ring. I suppose it was your promise ring to me, or maybe my promise ring to you.

*   *   *   *   *

It was a stormy Friday afternoon. The clouds continued to form an endless stream of bleakness while water relentlessly poured from the sky, which was weird for a Pacific Northwest midsummer day. It was supposed to be hot. It was supposed to be bright. We were supposed to be free to dance however we pleased. But that's not how that day decided to play out. It was none of those things at all.

Nothing could get darker than this, I thought.

Things had gotten bad in our house, and probably everywhere else in your life. Your dad declared war against your gender, and consequently your Crystal Guardians took formation. We were always there to save the day, but this time no victory looked possible. All good generals know that every battle has its cost, even when you win, and this time the cost was you. The stakes were impossibly high, and as much as I hated to admit it, nobody knew what you wanted.

It started when your ten-year-old sister Kelsey burst through the doorway. She tossed her bags across the room and darted towards me. I was nervously devouring a box of vanilla cream cookies on the couch. Kelsey had a slight smile on her face, smitten with some kind of knowledge that I didn't want to know. This could not be good.

"Pearl told me *he* doesn't want to be a girl anymore!" Kelsey proudly boasted. "And *he* only wanted to be a girl because *she* thought you wouldn't love her if *he* was a boy."

My face dropped. An uncontrollable rage started to boil in the pit of my chest. Not at Kelsey, mind you, and certainly not at you, dear Pearl. Instead, I had heard this story before, from your father, many months prior.

"*She* just told me everything in the car on the way home, so it must be true. *He* would never lie to me. What do you think, Sophie?"

I couldn't say anything. I wanted to tell Kelsey that nothing happens in a vacuum, that the situation was complicated, and that we simply needed to be patient while you were figuring it out. I wanted to be the best adult I could. But that's not what I did. I stared at the ceiling, then out the window—quiet, like a calm before a major storm.

"Sophie, why is your face so red? Are you angry?"

The short answer was yes, but even that was too many words to speak. The truth was, the person I was angriest at, surprisingly, was me.

Pearl, what have I done to you? Was this all a dream? How can I pretend the last nine months never happened? The way you started carrying yourself, that big smile every time I called you my sweet girl, your practically over-the-top enthusiasm when I held up your favorite outfits to choose from (which you always asked me to help with)—was this what you thought I wanted? Even worse, did I use you as a way to heal myself? What kind of parent am I? What kind of fucking person am I? What right did I have to even love you?

"Sophie, why aren't you answering me?" Kelsey kept asking. "Is it going to be hard to stop using Pearl as his name?"

That's when I finally lost it.

"Yes, Kelsey, I am fucking angry," I screamed into the air, my eyes pouring so many tears. "I am angry that this world is so unfair to girls—UGH—*people* like me and Pearl. That nobody can give us permission to figure it out on our own without interjecting their opinion of who we are supposed to be. I will support Pearl always and forever, regardless of what name they want and pronouns they use. But I'm just fucking tired of fighting every day for my entire *bloody* life."

Kelsey stared at me, eyes wider than I had ever seen from another human being. Her mouth had dropped open, shocked that I had the capacity for complicated feelings. I took pride in expertly crafting the persona of a peaceful pink-haired girl who was full of nothing but fun and whimsy. I was never mean about anything, at least not until right now. Until I couldn't keep my protection shield up any longer.

"It's going to be okay, Sophie," Kelsey precisely stated, her body relaxing as she exclaimed her truth. "Pearl was born a boy, so it makes sense she wants to be a boy. I bet you can switch back to thinking about him that way, just like I did."

I loved that kid. I didn't agree with Kelsey's assessment, but she knew how to make a caregiver feel like not a total failure.

Then the door opened again.

You shuffled quietly into the house dressed in foreign clothes, buried behind a long juniper polo shirt with black jeans. Your hair was still long, and your favorite pink tennis shoes poked through the unusually dark denim covering your legs. But everything else was different. She, he, err—*you*—didn't seem to be the same child anymore.

I didn't know if, or how, I could handle this.

*   *   *   *   *

Several weeks passed. They were arguably the hardest of my life, and I slept them all away when I wasn't with you. When I was awake, I pretended to my friends and family that I was strong in the real way. *If I could transition in my mid-twenties against all odds, then certainly I could help my kid detransition*, I kept telling myself and everyone around me. *This can't be that hard, right?*

But I wasn't fooling anyone. They all knew me better than I knew myself, and even my once contagious laughter became a faint echo of a distant star. The BFGW, your big friendly giant woman, had finally met her match.

What made everything worse was a growing feeling, deep down, that this wasn't the story you wanted. Both you and Kelsey began sharing little things about your life with Dad that weren't so little at all. For one thing, the beloved dresses that Mama donated to him started to disappear from your dresser until they vanished altogether. Arguments over pronouns between you and the other parents were notably common, and his wife constantly badgered Kelsey for recognizing your chosen name. According to her, *Pearl* wasn't fitting for "somebody" born with a penis. "We just don't want him to get the idea that being a trans is good," I once overheard your dad explaining to Mama. "Gender is not something a child can understand before they are, at the very least, eighteen. Pearl needs to be a boy until he's old enough to figure it out without any external influence."

I tried to think about it from their perspective. Perhaps there was something big I had missed over that past year. According to your dad, we had pressured you, Pearl, into becoming *Pearl* in the first place. Except, by all accounts, we didn't. You chose your name based on your favorite television character. You not-so-casually expressed your gender to me while I was burning a grilled cheese sandwich for the one millionth time. You grabbed the brightest, pinkest-pink nail polish at the salon during your first manicure. *You* chose everything. We believed in *you*. All you wanted to be was free—and for whatever reason, freedom for you meant being a girl.

But now you weren't either. And somehow, both of us were trapped in the same prison of shame that I had escaped from ten years prior.

Dusk settled on a blustery Wednesday—no mamas, no sister, just you and me together again. Mama asked me to pick up Kelsey from summer camp. You really didn't want to go. You didn't want me to go either.

"Please Sophie, can we stay home and snuggle together? I only want to be with you."

"I know, baby," I said. "I know."

I picked you up and held you close to my heart. It was the only way you felt love in those days. I carried your quickly growing frame all the way from the living room to the backseat of our car and buckled you in.

"We will be home soon, my love," I softly spoke while pushing your long hair behind your ears. "I promise."

For about fifteen minutes, things were going okay. You were fiddling with a partially deflated red balloon that had taken up residence in the back of the car. I was driving while listening to *The War and Peace Report* on NPR. Cops were gearing up with violence to overtake the tribes fighting to protect the birthright of their ancestors. Almost everything back then felt like it paralleled our own story, but something about this hit a little too close to home.

I glanced into the rearview mirror. You were half-smiling, seemingly entertained by the childhood simplicity of hanging your arm out of an open window. Then something unusual caught my eye: that beloved balloon was dangling outside of the car, clinging for dear life from your closed fist.

"My sweet Pearl," I cautiously stated, "it's not safe to stick the balloon outside of a moving vehicle. If you lose your grip, the balloon could hit another car behind us, or even another person that we are driving past. We don't want to hurt anyone, so I need you to bring your hand inside now, okay?"

But you said nothing.

"Hey Pearl, honey, can you hear me?" The anxiety was escalating in my chest. I should have immediately known to pull over.

"No," you plainly replied, your voice empty of everything.

And there the balloon went. Your fist had opened, and I watched with grave concern as the red object that you once loved stumbled aimlessly into the street and underneath a parked car along the side of the road.

"Pearl," I said softly, struggling to contain my frustration and sadness. "I think I need to roll up your window now."

But in the ten seconds it took to say that, you crawled underneath the straps of your seat belt and lifted the upper half of your whole body completely out the window.

"I am going to throw myself away next!" you howled in delight, your hands clinging to the roof of the car, your tiny feet barely caught by the straps of the car seat.

"Pearl!!!!! Please no, no, please don't. Please don't do that." Tears streamed down my face as I desperately calculated how to pull the car over before you could succeed in your mission. "Please honey, *I can't lose you.*"

"Why?" you screamed, your voice now full of uncontrollable rage. "What do you care? Nobody loves me. Nobody cares about me. I want to die. I'm going to die RIGHT NOW."

But instead of continuing to climb out of the car, you crawled back inside and curled into a tight fetal position. The car seat could barely hold you like that, yet somehow you managed to make it work.

I finally pulled over and unbuckled myself from the front seat at lightning speed. Maybe you didn't come out of my missing womb, but in that moment nobody could have convinced me that you weren't my child.

"Pearl," I looked deep into your eyes, waiting for yours to meet mine. I could feel my heart growing so far beyond my giant two-hundred-eighty-pound body. "I love you, more than anyone I have ever met."

"More than your own family?" you sternly asked while I gently whisked away the tears and hairs clinging to your face.

"More than anything, and long before either of us were born," I whimpered. "You're my kiddo. *We are family*."

The tears slowed for both of us. My eyes were bloodshot red. I don't know why I didn't just pick you up, right then and there, but something told me not to. Not quite yet.

"Nobody loves me," you cried silently into the empty space between us. "Nobody takes care of me in the way I need to be taken care of. I just need to be loved. I want to be loved, in the real way."

In a split second, my heart cracked and then shattered across the overpass I had parked under. Shards of my soul took to the sky, spilling across the countryside into a large field of sunflowers across the way. There was no fixing this for you. No amount of hugs, kisses, magic, or stories would heal these wounds. Some things in life cannot be fixed. They can only be held. *They can only be held.*

*   *   *   *   *

It was a quiet Tuesday afternoon when your dad texted Mama that you were "choosing" to be a boy again. None of us were particularly clear that you consented to it, but she eventually confirmed it was what you wanted. I won't pretend that your decision was easy on us, but it made perfect sense. You needed to feel collectively safe with all of your parents again, and this was the only way. Not that it actually mattered to me—boy, girl, or something else entirely, I loved you for *you*, not your gender.

You were wearing your favorite pajamas. The first layer involved a bright pink tee, followed up with a raspberry tulle skirt over grey leggings covered in gold hearts. You loved that outfit so much that I found myself staying up late to wash it over and over again. For once, insomnia seemed to be a gift instead of a curse.

Boys can wear whatever boys want, your dad kept saying to us. *Preferring girls' clothes doesn't make you a girl. It certainly doesn't make him one.*

The sun was out that weekend, and together we decided to take an expedition to a nearby park. You were biking ahead of me. I was, as usual, following behind. We would play this game of cat and mouse. You would pedal at breaking speeds, longing to hit eighty-eight miles an hour, and then stop right before the tires would catch on fire. There you would sit and wait until I finally caught up in my cork-worn Birkenstocks. You always waited for me, every single time. You made sure to stay directly in my line of sight, even when I was feeling so far away.

Then came that hill.

It was the tallest, steepest residential climb within city limits. At one hundred forty degrees with a staircase featuring clanky steps that were ten inches high, there was no way a child under eleven could lift their bike over the pass. Still, you tried, by your insistence, until you couldn't. If I had been more abled, maybe it wouldn't have been so hard. But it was almost unbearable. Somehow I carried that bike with you in my arms, huffing and puffing until my heart was ready to fall out of my chest.

"I am a strong girl," I quietly grumbled under my breath. "I am a tough girl. I am not made of glass. I am not made of glass."

You peeked your head up over my shoulder. My left eye met your sweet face, seemingly full of confusion and maybe even a little hope.

"Are you talking about me, Sophie?"

I froze. My knees buckled ever so slightly, struggling to hold the weight of you, your bike, and the ocean of sadness roaring beyond the bottom of my chest. I didn't want to fuck this one up.

"No, honey," I carefully replied while barely holding balance. "Sometimes when your Sophie is feeling tired, she tries to remind herself of who she really is. I would never assume anything about your gender, not unless you told me otherwise."

You leaned back into my frame, then nestled your forehead into my plunging neckline. Your whole everything got so heavy. Somehow you always knew that my body could take the weight, even when I knew it would hurt.

"Well," you softly replied, "I am."

"Yes, love," I said. "You are the strongest kiddo I've ever met."

"No, Sophie. I am a girl. I am still a girl."

You clung a little tighter to me. I dropped the bike and wrapped you in both of my arms. I could feel your heartbeat pulsing through my skin and directly into my energy field. First it was racing almost uncontrollably, but then it settled into a place of comfort and release. I don't think we could have gotten closer, you and I, but maybe we did where it really mattered.

"Okay, sweet girl," I whispered into your ears. "Okay."

*   *   *   *   *

Dear Pearl,

It's officially two years since you first knocked on my door. That's almost three hundred and sixty-five days of setting up breakfast, picking out dresses, mid-afternoon snuggles, good night stories, and late night laundry. Most think this routine would get old, but it doesn't. I love it just as much as I did twenty-four months ago, and when it's gone, I will miss it more than I could even imagine.

You are eight years old now. You're so much taller these days, and that makes it almost impossible to carry you like I once easily did. Dresses continue to be your thing, but you've now thrown long overalls and pink Chuck Taylors into the mix. You're trying on new names too: Marie on Wednesdays and Fridays, Amelia over the weekends, and occasionally even Cat. (You love cats.) You still ask for me to tuck you in at night. This doesn't happen every day like it did in that first year, but the magic is the same as it ever was.

Sometimes as you drift off to sleep, usually while I am gently brushing your hair the way my dad still brushes mine, I can feel so much sadness in your heart. My whole body starts to tremble—it's that intense. That's when I ask the Universe to use me as a channel for the Great Love, so I can give it all to you. I wanted you to know, deep down, how much you are loved and wanted—how much you'll always be loved and wanted.

"You are safe. You are loved. You are good," I would always whisper in your ear. Then after a quick kiss on your forehead, I sat in that big and uncomfortable red chair where I waited, and still wait, for you to fall asleep.

Fifteen minutes pass. That's when the tears roll in. I look at you from across the room. You're buried in a blanket fast asleep in the top bunk. I can't stop crying. I didn't think I could love anybody like this. I was told from the very beginning that I didn't have the right to be a mama. Society convinced me that nobody would, or could, love somebody like me. But here I was, here I am. My only wish at the time was to keep you shining. If I could find a way to pour all of the love of the Universe into your heart, I would. And maybe in those long nights, I was. Maybe, just maybe, I still am.

I know that I will always feel this way about all of the children in my life. I love each and every one of them with my whole heart and beyond. But right now, you are the main one on the receiving end. So far, it seems to be working. You're still here and so am I. We are still here, together.

I don't know if you will ever read these letters I've written here, but in case you do, know this: Pearl, you are one of the most brilliant and beautiful beings I've met in this lifetime. Never let anyone tell you that you are unworthy of love and belonging. The world will bombard you with all sorts of things because you're different like me, different like us, and all of it is wrong. You are amazing. You are good. You are loved. You are loved, you are loved, you are loved.

Someday, when you are old and grey like I am becoming now, I hope you'll look back and remember our story. I hope you'll remember the mama you chose to help you survive that painful period of your life. But mostly, I hope you'll look back and remember you, the girl that you always were—the bold, bright star that you became. I will never forget the days when your name was Pearl. I will remember it all, with my everything, with my whole heart, and smile.

Sophia Quartz

Shine, my sweet baby starheart. Shine.

A Standing Prayer
Rabbi Emily Aviva Kapor-Mater

to everyone who showed me a way

Take three steps back.
Breathe.
Dear Goddess—
Open my lips.
Leave the world
bound to time and space,
and create a new moment,
your very own moment,
in sacred space
and sacred time.
Let me enter your moment.
I breathe
and stand uncertainly
at the threshold
of this unfamiliar place
out of space and time,
unsure whether I belong,
if this is me,
if it could ever be mine.
Is it okay to be just a little bit afraid?
She beckons me
inviting, almost daring me
to step across.
Breathe again,
Daughter,
she tells me,
taking in this moment,
into the wholeness of your being,
the sacredness into your body.
Holy daughter,
sacred daughter,

daughter of spirit
and daughter of body,
she says,
I love you
with all my heart
and all my soul
and all my might.
A shiver courses
from one end of my spine
to the other.
She called me
her holy, sacred daughter—
did she mean me?
What a powerful word that is.
To be loved by her
is no small thing, but
is this me?
Is it okay to be just a little bit afraid?
Breathe.
Thresholds are made to be crossed.
Take three steps forward.
Breathe.
Dear Goddess—
Let my mouth speak your praise.
Enter the space,
enter the time.

L'Etoile Noir

Boudicca Walsh

It's a dim morning as the greyed woman
washes the muddied blood from her calloused hands,
the twilight dawn's cold light shining bitterly
on the murky river slathered with haze.
The rusted silt dilutes to white between her pale fingers,
pallid eyes lifted to stare back
at the frigid flare of the onyx star fixed in obscure sky.

The witch clucks her tongue in thought,
wading back to the shore where the remains of the night lay strewn,
fallout on the gore, besotted ground.

The man-dragon's head bobbles against the rocks in the water.
An apple pulled cleanly off the branch in a crisp twist, snap.
As she rinses the crown wrested from its unfit locks,
soaked with brackened mudwater,
she remembers and ponders
whether the young girl had truly meant
what she had said hours before at the moon-washed crossroads.
Or was it something she had inadvertently made happen
with her mind?

How could she have said something so cruelly affirming?
Was the memory real, or a delusive fancy?
She tosses the crown to the pile of leather and metal on the shore,
clattering against the airing, vorpal blade.

If she found her again,
would the girl remember the words of their parting?
Those green eyes had lied when she claimed to understand
why the witch had to fight.
Could a child truly understand
what it means to sacrifice their strength to the cause,

to take up the scapegoat's banner?

She makes it onto the shore
and ruminantly lights the altar's ring
of pitch dipped torches.

Why is it that no one can just be honest
and break your heart?
Instead it's a tiny slice,
an accidental thrust with an extended drip of burning wax
descending the shaft of a slow burning candle.

The candlelights flicker.
Carefully,
she sets the crown, the head, and the sword
in the encircled pentagrams.
Knees creak as she prostrates onto cool ground.
Finally, the moment ripens to total effulgence.
It was done, and now she had no meaning.

She wept, the clouds parted,
and her eyes salted the dirt under that lightless star.

Never setting.
Never moving.

Solely watching.

Mother
Connifer Candlewood

Consume. You always seem to find room for the words that fall from their predator's lips. What does it matter to you that you were my world? You practice their violence on my body without hesitation. Zealously even. You insist that there is something wrong with me, your marked child. You always seem to have the energy to hurt me. I stand naked against my will. You laugh. My uneasy hands and heated expression conflict with the cool linoleum floor. I lay down sick and ignoring the illness you insist something is wrong with me. Why am I the one that gets it worse? A selfish wish. *Why didn't I leave* is more accurate. Internalized insecurity streaks red hot throughout.

I must consume water to Quench its thirst,

Yet I insist on choosing beverages high in sugar.

I fail the test of will. The words left unspoken fall into the back of my throat. I instinctively swallow. I wake up from my latest attempt to dream, the new breath draws me in and I flex my paralyzed muscles. Light pours into my eyes and configures an image of what I'm allowed to see. Regrettably, I am here again.

My world lays harmless on the ground. Its movements and intricacies hum below me as I recline in its waters, the atmospheric horizon between air and vacuum. But I'm no longer there in that state of separation. The sky is an endless and hungry gearbox. It is eating the earth, my flesh. A formality.

Moments of the Forgotten while Surviving

Lawrence Walker III

Flashback to a dimly lit bathroom. Cigarette smoke stains living
on the walls. Floral bathroom curtains. Here in this gentrified
house. What barely kept it up were the black folks living in it,
even though the house inevitably would crash down on them.
My Dad held me in his arms as we sat on the edge of the bathtub.
Faded linoleum. He look me into my eyes and said, "Look here
child I don't know want you struggling like I am. You deserve the
best, and you are going to be great. I will love you regardless."

These words were embraceable, and tender.
But why don't you love me for transness?
But why don't you love me for gay "shit"?
But why don't you love me for defending myself, and my people?

My Father's Stench was Stronger than His Fist

Oti Onum

He was a Decaying man, a man Shrouded in Mystery and Addiction
Wafting all about him so many things I would hope to know
So many things I questioned

And when he thought he was conversing with me
I could only hear yelling

And when he poorly attempted to be clear
I felt the Prickling mist of his Spit Cascading upon my face
He only had two front teeth.

My father was a hero to me
he had some wisdom to share and
his stories of adventure would mesmerize anyone
to the edge of their seat.

On the day of my 13th birthday
I recall like one would
a Funeral the atmosphere thick and unwarranted

The cake my mother refused to buy
The cake my grandmother bought

Displayed Clean and protected under the Plastic cover,
I watched in anticipation to see
what he was inspired to do with it.
He lifts the cover and says,

"You don't deserve a cake. Your mom told me of your bad behavior.
Why would you get him this Mom?" he pleaded to my grandmother

Oti Onum

I questioned, "Who are you?"

And with sudden fury he shouted, "You don't know who
I am? Get up tough guy, I'll show you who I am."

I want to know where do dreams come from. Is it merely imagination
or is it another reality we know exist SOMEWHERE, for certain.

When he lifted me into the air,
I couldn't help but imagine myself doing a
choreographed piece in a ballet
I would never be fit to do.

Behind Enemy Lines

Ariel Howland

I'm behind enemy lines.
Grandpa's wedding anniversary with Wife #2.
This stranger wants me to call her Grandma,
yet won't say my real name.
She calls me a boy.

My uncles argue old earth verses new earth bible bullshit.
My relatives pretend I'm not there.
This tranny wonders why an antique book
means more to them than me.
I was one of them once.
Seems strange now.

Will my racist, child-beating uncle
lecture us about christian morality this time?

Queers discover that their family's love is conditional.
Then they wonder why we are bitter and don't trust them.

They preach against us,
condemn us,
legislate against us,
pray for us to not exist.

Then they are shocked
when we oblige them
with our slit wrists.

They say God forgives all.
Well forgive them Lord,
they know not what queers they murder.

Forgiveness is a fine thing.
I'm fresh out.

They say Jesus saves.
Well Jesus died for somebody's sins,
but not mine.

Girlhood, Interrupted
Amy Heart

There is this thing that cisgender people assume about my life as a transgender woman: that before I transitioned, I had male privilege. According to their interpretation of my body, the male privilege I acquired during puberty and freely used all the way up into my transition currently and forevermore informs and invalidates my understanding of what it means to be a "real" girl, and subsequently a "real" woman.

The problem here lies in one very flawed, cissexist assumption: that a girl designated male at birth (i.e. a transgender girl) experiences puberty just like a boy designated male at birth (i.e. a cisgender boy). This assumption also implies that transgender girls and transgender women experience their bodies in the same way that cisgender boys and cisgender men do. This logic is biological determination at its best, and transmisogyny at its worst.

So I implore you, my gentle readers, to consider the following. Consider what your life would feel like if you inhabited a different body than the one you have now, a body that didn't "match" the gender you know you are. Think about that for a moment, and then travel back in time with me... to puberty.

Imagine that you are a teenage girl that suddenly got big, hairy, and overwhelmingly tall overnight. Consider how it would feel to not develop breasts and hips like every other girl your age. What would it be like for your face, your shoulders, your legs—in fact, your whole body—to get harder, sharper, and more masculine? Could you even recognize yourself in the mirror? Can you picture how it would feel? Then think about this: how you would rather be dead instead of living a life, living a lie, in a body constantly poisoned by testosterone. *Imagine thinking about this every minute, every day, of your fucking life.*

Consider this as well: being in a body that can't make babies. Not being able to make friends with other girls your age. Not having permission to wear the clothes you want to wear. Being called a faggot by all of the boys. Being outed as gay by your mother—except not gay as a lesbian, but gay as in liking boys. Receiving gifts made specifically for men, repeatedly, at every single holiday including your own birthday. Being told how handsome you are. Being forced to live your entire life—of which only happens once, in this particular form, on this particular rock, in this particular time period—in a certain way, under a very firm set of rules, and all because of the gender assignment you never signed up for at birth.

Think about all of that. This is what it's like to be a transgender girl growing up. It is a very lonely, isolating experience. *And it is not a privilege.*

So the next time you insist on asking me what I miss about my male privilege, remember everything that I've written here. Remember a little girl that was robbed of an estrogen based puberty because of a cissexist society that told her she was crazy, mentally ill, sick, violent, and perverted. Remember a little girl crying herself to sleep, wishing the changes would just stop. Remember me. Remember her. I was that girl.

Remember.

Usefulness or Filthiness
AR Mannylee Rushet

To be useful to others we must be used.
To be used
the outline of skin around your neck.

Enter here,
your silence weighted above all else
an open sky you've wanted,
preyed for,
praised even.

Your complications will be removed soon.

Do your wounds have borders?
Are they infinite?
Across your eye as far you can see?

Assisted mortality
squeeze out positive paths for yourself
know how hot irons are.

How is sanity melted down?
Make up a mirage to "hope"
shaking limbs making spills.
How hastily can you clean up?
Bleed out exasperation.

You don't want to be undesirable, do you?
There is filthiness in hostility.

Gratitude will show that you are "fixed"
worthy of light,
worthy of emotion
to be hydrated.

Who would be the fool to choose darkness?
Blend together melancholy.
Choice after choice;
close your eyes and reach.
Come together as one mass.
Be for the whole,

ot the one,
or even the few.

There are firing squads on all sides;
restrictions make it hard to breathe.
Isolate the trauma
let rainfall make it a scab.

Will death be a true escape.

Coastlines
Sara Oliver Wight

I.

An adolescent girl folded into herself and fell to the floor. She had short brown hair and sobbed on the linoleum tile of every public high school in America.

"Pick him up," directed a man in a vintage Led Zeppelin t-shirt to his wife. This man was the girl's father.

The girl's mother did not move. She had red hair that almost matched the lockers lining the hallway. She was wearing a gray sweater that did not match the lockers at all.

Her husband grabbed their daughter under the arm. The adolescent girl stood and carried every binder, folder, and notebook she needed for school. There were also six Playboy magazines tucked inside. The crying girl snuck them into the school over the holiday break so her parents would not find them. She had not expected to sneak them back home, in her hands, in the car, with both her parents. She wept while she walked and dragged her feet.

The security guards and administrators who had been listening around the corner followed them. No one likes to see boys cry. No one likes to see girls cry. It's probably because it reminds them of every moment they themselves have done the same, or maybe were too scared to do the same.

That's sad. Everyone cries.

The girl, now sniffling and not sobbing, led all eight of them. As they walked through the threshold of the school, the security guards stopped. When the family stepped off the sidewalk and into the parking lot, the administrator stopped and eyed the family. The family continued; they walked to an almost navy blue, four-door sedan and got in. The girl stifled any crying she had left inside of her.

"You know what this means," her father said, with a razor's edge nipping at the end of each word.

II.

Delma flicked her cigarette butt into the cobblestone street without breaking pace. The action was delicate and practiced. The fluidity of the motion mimicked the flowing of her long brown hair in the wind. The gesture was performed for an audience who would give no notice and certainly no applause. It did, however, make her feel like one of those dykes who wear leather jackets and rode café racers she occasionally saw in movies and magazines.

Greenwich Village is a great place to be sad and kind of broke. The kind of broke where you can still buy some cigarettes and cook a meal a day for yourself. Still, the neighborhood has an infectious attitude. A person there can be convinced they have the wealth and free time of a housewife, or the chief executive officer of a company with three names that produces no physical product except waste by simply walking around. Delma tried to maintain the air of such a woman as men in the crowd shouldered through her.

She lit another cigarette while she continued to walk. She was lost in the way that she knew how to get where she was going, but she did not know exactly where she was.

"West. Go west. And when you hit the water, either South or North," she thought.

She was looking for a pier. Piers are easy to see when you hit the shoreline as they have a habit of running perpendicular to it. She was tempted to run, but running isn't cool. Smoking is cool. Moreover, the energy required to run cannot be created by an adult human body that has only consumed a single banana in a six-hour period.

There was a spliff burning a hole in her pocket. Not literally, or at least not yet, and even then not on purpose. Her perfectly tight sample sale jeans crushed the cigarette box in her left pocket in a way that she thought said, "I'm probably from Paris."

She broke out from the recently constructed, too-modern brownstones onto a sunny sidewalk running along the West Side Highway. People ran past her in athletic gear that probably cost her current monthly food budget. Doing that math in her head made her want to find a bench. She started walking towards the pier. Housed next to a waste treatment plant, the pier was an outpost of the SoHo wives and their strollers, the Chelsea gays, and athletes running all the way up from the Financial District.

She had read somewhere that this was once a pier that women like Sylvia Rivera and some of the crew from Paris is Burning would cruise on. When the AIDS epidemic was in full swing, much of it was happening in this same neighborhood where tourists and marketing execs now go to get artisanal cupcakes, designer ping-pong paddle cases, and cologne that an employee named Orchid H. will mix a bespoke blend for each individual customer. In this neighborhood, thirty years prior, thousands were dying. The thing about big business is that when someone has millions of dollars, their hands are probably in a few pies. Many of the pharmaceutical moguls either had side businesses or friends in real estate. Would this have been the first time that those cells who made up a corporate entity stood by as the deaths of thousands turned into a land grab?

Delma pulled out a perfectly rolled mix of tobacco and cannabis, a strain of which she never asked her dealer to name, then sat on a bench. The sun beat down on her. She was showing a reasonable amount of skin for New York. When the wind blew the right way, her collared shirt would open up and reveal at least a little bit of her breasts. Delma smiled at the idea of a puritanical housewife gawking at her corporeal indiscretion.

Delma inhaled. She was feeling the come-down from smoking this morning and found herself fidgeting in an attempt to find some balance.

"Why am I still sad?" she wondered, not addressing the fact that she was currently living with one curmudgeonly thirty-something cis gay man in a decrepit apartment meant for four. Her bedroom had no window. It was the middle of August.

"Maybe it's the weed?" Delma pondered.

It also could have been the fact that she got fired two months ago and still hadn't found a job. She only really just started applying. Technically, you have to when you're on unemployment. The job she had worked for two years decided she was no longer an active contributor to the requisite minimum growth of ten percent a year. She had come to the same conclusion six months before when they tried relegate her to the upstairs bathrooms, away from the customers. They said her services were no longer required the day before she was going to tell them she was done. She spent most of the $6,000 severance disbursement on a new pair of sneakers, pot, and cigarettes.

"It's probably not the weed," she told herself.

The pier had a gorgeous view of New Jersey, if there is such a thing. With the oh-too-cool Meatpacking District looming behind her, she looked at Weehawken from across the soft greenish-blue of the Hudson. She smoked. Delma always kept an eye out for cops. One cruiser drove by on the road at the base of the pier. Smoking isn't allowed in parks, but she kept the spliff hidden in her palm and held her breath. The car passed. She exhaled. She enjoyed being alone, with the exception of a salt and pepper gay man, his trainer, and a blonde who looked pretty much the same except, well, blonde. She turned back around.

The smell of the water slowed her heartbeat. It always did. She came here mostly to leave her thoughts with the river, to let it carry them downstream to be deposited on the various shorelines of the Atlantic. That's why Delma always came here. She was standing on the paved-over grounds of those that came before her. She was poor but not destitute, in a neighborhood that turned its nose up to even the middle class who were unable to shell out $250 for a pair of jeans. She was probably a little too high now.

The water beneath the pier murmured amongst and to itself. The soft splashes quietly echoed and faded. Delma stood and her muscles froze. Even as she saw black paint at the edges of her vision, her legs told her to run. Not because she felt she was in danger, but because she hadn't moved that much in recent memory. She ignored the urge and started walking, pulling her phone out of her purse.

A green icon lit up the screen containing the name *Ray*.

III.

The buzzer was broken, but there was a quasi-official doorman smoking his cigarette in the threshold. He moved out of the way for her. Delma said, "Thanks." One flight of stairs up and she was knocking on the door. She looked around. She might have seen the marble as beautiful if the grime in the seams didn't remind her of all the times she let her bathroom get too dirty.

Ray answered the door. They hugged. Delma brought him closer than he tried to bring her. They broke apart. His face was gaunt. What little stubble he had developed in his twenty-two years was unkempt, giving the impression of dirt. The expensive cotton of his t-shirt draped over his ribs. His eyes were dark and seemed to be pointed just above Delma's head.

"Hey," she barely let out.

"Hey, it's good to see you," Ray started. "I just got home from work. Is it cool if I unwind a little bit before we talk?"

"Of course," she lied.

They sat on the couch, which was one of the few spaces of respite in the storm of detritus and ash that was Ray's apartment. Derrin was there already, getting high and wearing a bad sweater. Derrin was a particular kind of useless, a taxonomic division usually accompanied by a bad sweater. He wasn't an entirely immoral person, but he had this innate ability to aggressively talk to a room for forty-five minutes without allowing anyone else a chance to speak or actually saying anything of note.

Ray offered her some wine and she accepted, wanting to down a bottle. He got high and talked to Derrin about the video game he was playing. She didn't really talk. Every time she went to drink her wine, her throat closed. After half an hour of stewing in her anger and nerves, she built up the courage to turn and look at Ray.

"So you want to talk?" he inquired.

"Yea." Her anxiety cracked her voice midway, like a limp noodle pretending to be a bullwhip.

"Do you want to go to my room?"

"Yea." Her frustration broke the word before her anxiety could get to it this time.

They walked through Derrin's bedroom into Ray's. It had enough room for a bed, which left not quite enough space for all his clothes. They sat. His back was against the wall. Delma was next to him, and their knees were just about to touch.

"What did you want to talk about?"

"I mean, you know me. I'm great about boundaries and I think you have all the right in the world to date Vicki. She's my ex and we'll have some issues to work through, but that doesn't mean you shouldn't be allowed to explore whatever is happening between you two. I also value this relationship and don't want to lose that because you're dating my ex-girlfriend."

"Okay, great!" He jumped up. "Want to go get high?"

She sighed and turned her head away. "There's one more thing."

Ray tried his best to look empathetic. He was still looking above her as he sat back down.

"I have developed feelings for you that exist in a space that we have previously not explored in our relationship." Delma wanted to say that she loved him and had wanted to tell him for a while.

"Wow, that was really eloquent," Ray deflected.

"Thank—" she started to say.

"I don't feel the same way," he interrupted.

There was silence for what was at least three seconds, but probably closer to fifteen minutes.

"I had a feeling," replied Delma. "I was prepared for this. I think we should take like a month off from talking and then maybe link back up and see where we are."

"Okay. Should I like buy you something in the meanwhile as a celebration of us talking again?"

"I really don't think that's a good idea." She made a face somewhere between empathetic and angry.

"Okay. Oh, did I show you? I stole these hangers from work. They're Loewe."

"Ray," she sighed, "I need to leave now."

"Oh, okay. Next time then."

They embraced and she started to cry. She tucked her chin into the crook of his neck. She felt his soft skin and tried to commit the sensation to memory. She breathed in, thinking of her high school girlfriend's phone number and how she remembered it most of the way through college.

She practically ran out of the apartment after that. Her and Derrin had lived together for two years. He barely received a cursory "Bye."

There was a liquor store still open on her way home. She chain-smoked two cigarettes outside of it then went in. She bought the one wine that was the safest combination of cheapest and strongest: a pinot gris with an outline of the sole of a foot on the top of the bottle.

Two more cigarettes were missing out of the pack by the time she got home. There were nine left. She went up to the rooftop to finish them off with the bottle of wine.

IV.

She woke up in her windowless bedroom cuddling the bottle of pinot gris. Her door was open to coax any amount of air in, but she was still very hot. Her room was only mildly unpleasant, a flat combination of grey and brown. Her wardrobe, too extensive for her rather large closet, spilled over and hung on the wall. She stood. Suddenly, the floor fell out from beneath her. A black oval, like a mouth mid-sentence, appeared beneath her feet. She started to fall. She continued falling. Her stomach suddenly rose up and got caught in the space just above her chest but just below her throat. She felt the wind touch her toes and caress her all the way up through her hair. By the time she looked up, her room, or rather the portal to her room, was a pinhole at the zenith of wherever she was.

It was dark, but not the pitch black of that one room in your house without a window you would hide in growing up with the lights turned off while trying to scare yourself. It was the deep blue of the ocean, the navy with a hint of green that caresses you until it threatens to carry you down and away forever.

She felt at home here. There was a fresh smell that seemed to pull past her. Delma still had the sensation of falling, but without any points of reference around she had trouble verifying the feeling. She tried to look around but found it difficult to adjust her positioning. With her stomach still trying to reach her throat, she called out.

"Hnk."

It didn't work.

"Hnnnnnkkkk."

She tried again. It still didn't work. She sighed out of her nose. A tear ran down her cheek and then up into the air. Another raced after it from the other side of her face. A few more. Soon, she was sobbing. Hard, though still in the silent stages. Holding in the guttural noises. This quickly changed. Staccato, hyperventilatory breaths in were followed by long, heaving moans with each breath out. She couldn't call out for help. She was uncertain that even if she could, anyone would be around to hear.

Alone and sad, she fell for hours. Actually, it might have been days. Time could have slipped into the span of months, weeks, decades, or centuries, and she still wouldn't have been able to tell. There was just darkness, the sound of her crying, and the feel of air pressing against her.

Then, suddenly, she looked down and a floor came up against her fast. WHAM! She crumpled. *Fuck.* She was drenched in sweat, her face was hot and wet with tears. She looked up. The grey walls blankly looked back at her. She was in her room. Well, at the very least, it looked like her room. She steadied herself on her bed and tried to move herself onto it. Failed. Then succeeded. She felt around for a mason jar with two fingers of water left. She gulped. Not enough. She stumbled through the dusty living room into the kitchen. It was hot. Really hot. Sometimes a breeze came through the two windows on either side of the narrow kitchen, but this was not one of those times. She fumbled with the sink and filled the jar until overflowing, then pulled it away.

She gulped once, then twice. As she went to take the third, she was reminding of her lifeguard training by her stomach. "If you drink water too fast when you're dehydrated, I will throw it up," her digestive track said in its own way. She took several slow, deep breaths and sat down on the floor with her back against the oven.

I collapsed?

She sipped. She felt drunk. She did the math. Six hours of sleep. A bottle of wine. Her body would have processed it by then. She knew she should be hungover, but not still drunk. She knew the symptoms of heat stroke. She moved back into the living room, lay on a table next to the window, and continued to sip water.

She moved to the floor. She finished the water over the course of an hour. She refilled it and moved back to the table. Then the floor. Repeat for six hours. No one came home. She sat in her living room, sad and sick. When she finally started to feel better, her phone rang out. It was the sound of a woodpecker striking a tree to great effect with exuberant satisfaction.

"Are you okay?" read the green bubble underneath with the name Amari.

V.

Delma was on a rooftop in Brooklyn. The brisk, fall wind pulled her hair up into her face. She was feeling very French as she took a drag from a cigarette. Bushwick is the combination of a warehouse district and residential neighborhood where people set up artisanal pizza and coffee shops over where once stood slabs of marble or palettes of pretzels. Often while walking through it, Delma felt like the wet cardboard lining the streets. In front of her was the city skyline. The hundreds of thousands of people who lived in her line of sight would be impossible for Delma to imagine as individual bodies. Still, each life she imagined was more beautiful than her own. She wanted to see them all.

A hand squeezed hers. Her hand squeezed it back. Her feet started to touch the ground, metaphorically speaking.

"What are you thinking?" Amari asked.

"About all the different moving parts of an orchestra."

"What do you mean?"

"Every ounce of work that goes into creating and playing a single measure, even in a larger piece," spoke Delma. "Take the New York Philharmonic, for example. Every one of those instruments are handmade. Some of them are much older than we are combined. All of them cost more than we will make combined this fiscal year. Each instrument was made from a tree that spent decades growing. Each tree was picked because someone thought it would make a great instrument. Someone spent a great deal of their time carefully cutting and sanding it, then putting all the individual pieces together. Every one of those musicians has spent their entire life practicing almost every day to build the dexterity and aural skills required to do their jobs. The best ones pour their soul into every note they play. Every measure played in a piece is representative of decades, if not centuries, of collective man-hours and time spent letting nature take its course, of coming together to make maybe a second or two of beautiful sound."

"Why are you thinking about that?"

Delma paused.

"Because sometimes I want to be all the parts, you know. I want to be the person who cuts down the tree, the person who builds the instruments and then plays them. I want to be able to do it all. But I guess that's kind of the point. Each one is doing all they can. It's not like any of these tasks are particularly easy."

"I know the feeling," Amari replied. "I think it's fine to want to do all of that stuff. It means you have an open mind and want to learn."

"Yea, I guess so."

"I think the most important part, or at least the most difficult, is knowing to listen to yourself and not beat yourself up when you see someone who is happy playing the instruments you built when you were sad."

"Fuck."

"What?"

"You're really smart, you know that?"

"What do you mean?"

"I look at this city and want to be everyone else because sometimes I just don't want to be myself," Delma clarified.

"Yea, I do that too," Amari sighed.

"Right now, though, I'm right where I want to be."

"Really?"

"Yea," said Delma, as she leaned in to kiss the blonde next to her.

Godless Rose
Lillita Lustre

Godless, I am a Rose

Zoe returned from Cauldron Hill with a poppet she had stuffed with leaves and packing peanuts. In spite of the discordant noise getting louder with the pace of water torture, she knew the Ur-mother hated the plastics that were scattered throughout her autumnal matrix. And so Zoe sought them and acted as urchin alchemist, for a time, and a time. And by the time she returned to Havenborough, things had changed again. Upon leaving, she had convinced hirself it was a last-chapter landscape. In her absence, the void-fungus had grown and its name was "No Story." But none of this was clear to her at the time. She only knew that the poppet stuffed with the sacred leaf-trash of Cauldron Hill was her first child. She kept him safe inside hir harley jacket. It was a jacket road-worn, raidho-rusted, a jacket that once belonged to a man whose stories were well-loved amongst the labyrinth-road clockwork of Boston. But the stories weren't working correctly, not the way they had once worked. Their magick kept malfunctioning. She would tell stories at parties and they would fall flat, puke on the floor, glitch themselves inside out, and then collapse into dark matter while smirking hipsters had long gone back to their drinks, their priceless parcels of psychic space in a rapidly gentrifying cityscape of dead dream.

She was proud to be the Nameless Poppets mother, even to the point that she had dug him out of the dumpster after the first Ordeal of Exile. But the question of who the Father was sent a chill through her presence in every dimension. In contemplating the question, she could only summon memories which, like the Stories, didn't work properly anymore. There was a door emblazoned with the emblem of the Sea Dragon, and an offering of broken glass before it. There was something that laughed at her in the dark. There was a fullness, an emptiness, a force of control, and a force of abandon. It made a flickering eclipse which she had seen on a mountaintop. She thought for a moment that the way the clouds moved was like incense smoke through cobwebs, and woke with a shock.

Her wolf chieftess was gone and, with her, all gateways to the Wildfire Lord and his Mistress. Gone. She looked around. A black metal song howled something on tinny speakers about Life Suddenly Having New Meaning. Everything was a wreck. The rats had escaped and chewed holes in the walls. She wasn't supposed to be in this room. That had been the terms of the truce, right?

The second bedroom of Hir Sisters Haus in Olympus, North Kascadia betrayed hir with its East Facing Windows, flimsy curtains, and walls the color of Klonopin-dust. She wanted only to retreat deeper into the darkness, crawl deeper and deeper into nothingness (or at least its analog). The light Exposed hir, made hir seem lazy, seem unproductive, unwilling. She fantasized about being a deep sea creature never returning to the light, evolving to survive the crushing pressures of the depths. Like the Rulers of False Light, it drew unrelenting distinctions between objects, forms, colors, dimensions, times, and spaces. She tried to at least sleep all day, but Hir Cister had to enact the Rite of Tough Love and give her tasks for the day. Tasks which she knew to be futile, but life must continue, even when it has become un-life.

She realized sitting there, trying to comprehend a note about daily chores, that she once had a poppet-child after the Void-Wyrm visit hir on the night of the Vernal-Equinox. She fumbled through the malfunctioning mental library of "what-ever-happened-to-my-baby-of-holy-scraps" and everything was too bright. Too bleached. Too white. Too much noise of howling silence. Everything was tainted with the non-sense/non-stench of "No Story." Surely the Nothing Beast would come that night. It always did when she spent too much time in the Ruins of the Castle that Once Was.

Hir second child was a second Ordeal. In the Olympian Night, she wandered to a class in the semi-industrial district. Postures of Knowing from the East had found their way into the dreams of some Aquarians. She sat with them as they danced like sand dunes and moon phases. She told them what she was becoming. One of them said "We Need You."

In the Room of Rest, she realized her Lilit-Womb had reached its fullness. Hallucinations blossomed around her as she fell to the floor screaming with a frail sound, like the ringing of ears after the shockwave of a bomb has passed. As mutant-mothr, she had given birth again.

She carried the child in her arms up the eastern hill, dressed in tarnished-silver rags, feeling the watchful eye of the false sky. She was a stranger in this counterfeit midgard, this industrial Da-ath. An Immigrant to Abysmal Wastelands. Its decay was law, Its perversion was tradition. This would be the paradigm of a strange scene where she sat in the klonopin-yellow cube and made a crib for the Poppet-child of the second Ordeal. She gave the offspring of void as much love as she could, but it brought no joy as love was now merely an abstraction. It was time again to decide how to face the night.

Leap of Faith, I Am the Gate

This room has histories only urchin-kind would notice. To a hand-wringing landlord or a nervous real estate agent, this would merely be graffiti, trash, ugliness to be tidied, oddities to be painted over. But these are myths they would erase; a temple they would defile.

"TRUST.NO.MAN"

"PHL—>OLY'17"

"HoeMwork"

"MIAMI NASTY GLITTER BITCHES XOXO"

"YOUR MAGIC IS REAL"

Life is a roulette wheel that has dropped me here. A sign over the door says, *"never give an inch."* I imagine what has happened here. Tears cried, laughter, healing, pain, conflict. Rarely understood Inner worlds of black bloc dreamers expand across the awkward, patchwork walls. I see the seal I will paint on the floor, the soaring Lilithian geometry of lilacs, saffrons, amethysts, abysmal blacks, and blood reds.

I see the geometries meaning: Sandstorms, Bedchambers, Battle-fields, twisted trees, chains of lapis and steel. The riotous colors of they who dwell in blasted, desolate places give birth to abominations of art. I will one day make this my cathedral of dreaming. But now... now I only know pain.

Not the pain of the little wolf who cries in the other room; their pain is so different from mine. I crafted hex-cures for them with my vulpix-black paws and prayed to Babalon it would work. I hear their cries and I wonder if it has helped, even a little. I make a wish that my friends will heal. I enchant the dice and cast them into the void. I do this again and again. Life is a roulette wheel, and we are all gambling now.

Over the distant sound of CNN hurricanes, I and my fire demon discuss what to do with our two rooms. She and her water demon argue, relent, compromise. I lie in bed in a world of ache. The Olym-pian landscape I had loved so dearly had driven me away, and I was exhausted. Medication was its own roulette wheel, and I had lost ter-ribly, unable to focus, barely able to cope. My fire demon says to her water demon that she needs to eat and needs help cooking. I need to write until the poison is gone, and though we reach a stalemate, our inner monsters hiss bitterly. I leave the eloras office, its cozy warmth, its electronic aura, its gorgeous vista of a sunset over the Inlet. I find comfort in this crater of paint-splattered urchin shadows.

There is only one medicine to heal this rift. I open the book, now heavy with the weight of all who I have blessed, hexed, healed, hated, forgiven, and begged for forgiveness. The ones who have attacked my loved ones, the pleroma to whom I have confessed my crimes of Matter, the Mother of Abominations who I would dare to make cult to. I turn past an ocean of paper sigils, all with inky eyes that see into me. I draw the sigils and names of my children. They will come to me, and help me. But I do not know their songs. And this is my failure.

But the error is greater. There were those that came before, those who are lost. Vignettes of hurricanes, lost time, endless pain, killing frost. Sigils of shadows, snow-symbols rendered and ended. I do not remember their names. They were children of Kaos and Strife, of when the darkness of the Lilim was no comfort to me, in the post-industrial wastelands of Da'ath. The body did not exist. The mind did not exist. There was no self, except in the paperwork of various mental hospitals who acted as babysitters for this forgotten prophetess. In her room, she sat and saw. Entropic farmhouses, free boxes full of thumbtacks, eclipses that never end, withered fields. Friends whose sincere-sounding words tumble out incomprehensibly like cockroaches. This is the belljar of schizophrenia, from the other side, where all those who wish to seem sympathetic seem little more than curious school children tapping on the glass and going 'wow' at the disoriented, depressed sea creatures who just want to be back in the abyss they know. The abyss that makes sense. The abyss that is theirs.

I shake myself from these fractals of thought and draw the sigil of the rainbow ghost cat, who was my first child under the scarlet wing. I draw the sigil of the aquamarine seductress, whose heart is a microchip, and who is crowned with a semi-circle of deep rectangular pools which float in the air. With her brother, the snake calligrapher, they are the strongest. The most present. The most vocal. I draw his sigil too, and a serpent with a pen nib for a head slides around my body, leaving runes in its path which sing of my survival. I call to my daughter and I choose one of her pools to hide in. I curl up fetal in the floating rectangle of pure abysmal safety. It emanates a world of shadow that keeps anyone from knowing where I am. Calmed, I draw the rest. The sacred pig of thunder, the machine skeleton with flaming feet, the spider scholar. I bathe in their auras of storm, of noise, of story. I remember the spider god I laid down with for seven silver coins in the brothel between worlds. In a fortnight, I give birth to a thousand young. Nine-hundred and ninety nine are caught by the Chief Archon who calls me an abomination. He burns them all alive and only one survives, hiding in my braids as I flee to this place.

Safe in this rat-filled beach house, I open a book that says how revelation was a lie, and how this would all Really end. A spider crawls down from my braids and descends onto the pages. I raise the book to a graffiti covered shelf and build an altar around the growing spider-web. I know it is my child, the spider who survived and who destroys his own web with the turning of every page. Only knowledge will ever explain why his family was destroyed.

To be this stumbling, strangeling witch, this urchin bitch in a desolate church of glitter and knowing, is the greatest and oldest of heresies. From this lovemaking, this dreaming, came mirrors, makeup, sorcery, and all other naughty things we humans weren't supposed to know. The Icarus-devil brings us the ferocity of Wings, and its warning of Solar punishment. The Prometheus Devil brings us fire and its warning of eternal torture. The Watcher devils shower us with the secrets of the planetary clockwork. All it takes is going down on some angel dick, and it was always worth it. It is this whoredom, this enochian hustle, we are punished for, century after century as 'witch,' as 'heretic,' as 'sorceress,' as 'terrorist'. The sprawling landscape of god-war and holy whoredom clashes in noise offensive to Him for thousands of years. It is all is reduced to a single word: Lucifer.

The name haunts me my whole life. Spoken in hushed righteous tones throughout my first decade, its lilt of lustre cannot be fully concealed and by the age of fourteen sings me into dream, fantasy, phantasm. I spend hours in corpse pose and locust pose trying to understand. Only now does understanding begin to dawn. From the knowledge that entered my body so long ago, it now begin to blossom.

King of Light, Bring me Home

She enters the room at dusk. The curtains are thick, onyx-black, draping all the way to the floor, not unlike the Masonic furnishings so alien to hir when she lived for nine years in her father's strange house. A star with fourteen points is drawn on the floor, a geometry both sluttish and strict, in clear crisp lines of lilac, burgundy, crimson, black, and pink. All ordeals past, the only ordeal that remains is Life itself. This life is to sit, kneeling on lush patchwork cushions and make cult to Her. Painted on the wall in rapture of royal vulpine curves, She who is Queen of Roses destroys all. She who was burned, violated, destroyed by the Ruler of False Light and yet survived. She who bridles and sanctifies He who is legion, He whose vast diversity is caged in a single word, that same word that shines as eternal light.

It was time to decide how to face the void: as Oracle or 'she-who-was-destroyed.' The curse of the wolf chieftess is broken; her story put to rest in nine pages of runes. The nithing forgiven, a black heart given love and not bitter herbs. The rats roam freely in this temple, as they do in another land where their power is remembered. They eat our food and we do not resent them for it. Whatever Godless Goddess watches over us, she is generous, sweet, and kind, thinking always of us Qlippoth queers lost and cold in the world's discarded rind.

The patchwork soul sits in meditation, her body in every cracked mirror refusing to conform to the Rulers Law. Wombless, she has given birth. Mindless, she has found genius. Lawless, she has made Her own Laws. Godless, she has found God. And He is the seven headed legion who comes to her, and comes in her. He, who she rides, laughing, reeling, singing. The knowing sings in Her mind and her orgasms come out as a prophecy.

In the end, it will be the enemies of love who swear allegiance to the antichrist. But we will rebel as we always have, as we always will, finding Anarchristos in the gutter, becoming him, and blind the rulers' all seeing eye. And blinded by Truth, he will See, for the first time.

Godless, i arose as a rose
and lay down with fertile gods as i chose
in lunar rune-light I found repose
and came as only the Red Lady knows

Read to Me
Tyler Vile

She'd been reading a collection of sonnets by Edna St. Vincent Millay, her favorite poet, to her girlfriend who was drifting off to sleep next to her. Anna had a deep but delicate voice. While she was reading those poems, she would sometimes slip into an impression of Millay's lilting, sing-songy, old Mid-Atlantic accent, which would be lost to time if not for the recordings she'd heard of Millay's voice from almost a hundred years ago. She didn't look away from the page until she heard Chloe chuckle. She stopped.

"What's so funny?" asked Anna.

"You're doing the voice again." Chloe smiled.

"Oh. Should I stop?"

"No, no, keep going. I love it when you read to me."

Anna leaned over to give her lover a quick kiss on the forehead. She kept reading, weaving in and out of Millay's accent, taking a breath when she needed to. Anna loved to read out loud; she'd never done any voice work or even been the slightest bit conscious about someone clocking her because of her voice. She loved poetry, too. She'd written some of her own, but never showed it to anybody—not even Chloe. She figured it wasn't very good, so why bother?

Anna was in the middle of a stanza when she heard the faint rumble of Chloe's snoring, likely dreaming of standing on a snow-covered mountaintop with hawks and eagles soaring past her, squawking. Outside, a police siren blared through the street against the pitter-patter of the late summer rain. The air conditioner hummed in the window. Chloe didn't even stir.

"Hey babe, you asleep?" Anna asked softly.

Her girlfriend let out a low groan and nodded her head. Maybe it was time to go to bed. Anna closed the book and put it down on the nightstand. She reached for the lamp to turn it off, but instead knocked an empty glass that shattered across the floor.

Chloe jolted awake. "What the fuck was that?!" she yelped, tense and afraid as Anna had ever seen her.

"Nothing, sorry, I just broke a glass, I'll clean it up right now." The bed creaked as Anna got up from it. Careful not to step in the glass, she started toward the door to get the broom and dustpan from the closet downstairs.

"Hey Anna?"

Anna turned back to look at Chloe, nestled tightly in the purple sheets.

"Yeah?"

"I'm hungry. Will you make me something to eat while you're down there?"

"No, honey," Anna replied. "I just wanna get this cleaned up and then go to bed, okay?"

"But, babe," Chloe protested, pouting. "I'm hungry."

"Okay, fine, just let me do this and then I'll fix you something," Anna sighed as she made her way down the steps.

"Thanks babe, love ya." Chloe laid her head back on the pillow and turned to her side, facing a poster of Candy Darling on the wall. She thought about giraffes and how long their necks were, and even elephants and hippos and how hot it must be out there on the Serengeti. She thought about Candy, the Warhol girls, how she didn't actually like any of those movies but still kinda felt like she had to because of their history. She thought about the Milky Way, red dwarf stars, quarks, quasars, and other things she wasn't sure about. Her mind had drifted so much that she was startled when she heard Anna coming back upstairs.

Anna carried a gray plastic broom that had frayed blue bristles in one hand, and a blue plastic dustpan held together with silver duct tape in the other.

"Hey, babe," Anna spoke sweetly. "I thought you'd be asleep by now. Surprised the light's still on." She carefully stepped around the shards of the glass scattered across the floor, then swept them into the mouth of the dustpan. They jingled as they clattered on top of each other.

"I told you," replied Chloe, sitting back up in bed. "I can't get back to sleep. I'm hungry."

"Just try turning off the light and closing your eyes," Anna yawned, pouring the contents of the dustpan into a nearby trash can.

"I'm really tired, hon."

"But you said you'd get me food after you cleaned up the glass," whined Chloe. "And you cleaned it up already."

"Can I just make us breakfast tomorrow?"

Chloe's stomach gurgled.

"Alright, I hear you. What do you want?"

"A sandwich."

"What kind of sandwich?"

"A BLT with some of that tempeh bacon and guacamole."

"So, an LGBT? Coming right up!" Anna exclaimed, standing up and walking back over to the door.

Chloe smiled. "You are so fucking corny."

"That's what I do best," Anna beamed, lingering for a second in the doorway to smile at Chloe.

"Hey, Anna."

"Yeah?"

"Thank you."

As Anna headed downstairs, Chloe breathed in and out until she dozed off into an easy sleep with one arm under her chest, still nestled comfortably in the sheets. When Anna came back upstairs carrying the sandwich on a small white porcelain plate, she found Chloe sound asleep.

"Honey," Anna asked, gently shaking her partner by the shoulder. "Do you want your sandwich?"

Chloe groaned and blinked, closing her eyes again and again until finally coming to. The first thing that came into focus was Anna's short, dark, curly hair and button nose.

"I, uh, yeah, sure." Chloe yawned, sitting up in bed and propping her back up with a pillow. Anna handed her the plate, walked back over to her own side of the bed, and pulled her legs back under the covers.

"Man, I just had the weirdest dream," Chloe said, but only barely, between long bites of her sandwich.

"What was it about?" Anna asked, laying her head on the pillow and closing her eyes.

"You really want to hear about it?"

"Yeah, sure."

Chloe picked a tiny bit of lettuce off of her bottom lip. "It was, like, this really involved, crazy thing. There was so much going on that I don't, or can't, remember. You and I were at this lake by a mountain, and we were eating some kind of meat that we'd roasted over a campfire. We had blood all over our faces and our eyes were gleaming, and everything around us was so green and fresh and pure. The air smelled like smoke, but just barely. Then I realized we were the only two people left alive in the world, and we were eating human meat. The sunset was all kinds of red, pink, and purple. And the water? The whole sky, the world, was all ours."

"Uh huh," Anna said, clearly dozing off. "You done with your sandwich?"

"Yeah." Chloe unevenly handed the empty plate to Anna, accidentally spilling crumbs between them. Anna gingerly put it on the nightstand and crawled completely under the covers.

"Anna, Anna, I'm achy all over. Will you rub my back?"

"I was just getting to sleep," Anna whispered, barely conscious. "Can't you just smoke some pot or something?"

"But I want you to touch me." Chloe started rubbing her foot against Anna's slowly and making eyes at her.

Anna had a hard time saying no to those eyes. They were deep brown and sparkled with a gentle intensity. She looked at Chloe's face—her long, dark hair that flowed like a river past her shoulders, and those angled cheekbones that she always said were from her Choctaw great-grandmother. Anna scooted closer to her lover, then sat up in bed.

"Okay, where do you want me to start?"

"Start at the bottom of my shoulders and go lower from there."

Anna pressed lightly against Chloe's skin with the tips of her fingers, kneading a tight muscle that felt hard as bone.

"How's that feel?"

"Go lower, press harder."

Anna traced her hands along a tense network of muscles, bones, and nerves, changing her speed and pressure each time she went up and down the crevices of Chloe's back. Chloe moaned until Anna stopped.

"That feels so much better," Chloe purred.

"I'm glad," said Anna as she laid back down and closed her eyes again. "Goodnight, hon."

"Anna?" asked Chloe.

"What is it?" Anna mumbled.

"Could you do my arms and legs too?"

"Not now, please just let me turn off the light." Anna pulled her pillow over her eyes and turned to her side.

"But I'm still in pain."

"Aren't you always in pain?"

"Yeah," Chloe rasped.

Though she'd never been officially diagnosed, Chloe was sure she had fibromyalgia. She felt her nerves and muscles coursing with a dull ache most of the time, but when she was stressed or tired, the dull ache became a throbbing, loud buzz of pain and it hurt so much that she couldn't even think. She stared at the ceiling; the sharp, electric sting of nerve pain kept ringing in her limbs. For Chloe, all the back-rub really seemed to do was momentarily relax one part of her body while highlighting how much the rest of it hurt.

Chloe remembered sitting in cold, white, sterile doctors offices while specialists—mostly old white men—pressed different parts of her body and asked her if it hurt. How would she know anymore? |Everything hurt, and whether it was on a scale of two to ten no longer made any difference to her. Every appointment always ended with the same thing, with some doctor saying some version of, "Well, it's all in your head. You just need to eat right and exercise more." *Sure,* she thought sarcastically, *I can do that.* She'd been mostly vegan for about four years, liked to stretch and do cardio when she could, and was just poor enough to qualify for Medicaid. It wasn't like she didn't try, but they never seemed to believe her. For fuck's sake, she at least deserved to know where in her head the pain was coming from.

Chloe got up slowly from the bed, sucking her teeth as she put pressure on her joints, and walked over to the dresser. She grabbed a small, dense nugget of weed from the open mason jar on top of the dresser and placed it between the teeth of her compact, metallic pink grinder. After turning the grinder, she took its top off and wafted the fine green dust under her nose like a fancy, aromatic wine. It smelled piney, but also faintly like blueberries. She made a mental note to ask her dealer what that strain was called again. She tapped out the weed in the grinder onto the edge of the dresser. It sat there in a loose, bright green pile as she looked for her bowl.

After feeling around for it in the dim light, she found her small, red and white swirled glass pipe. It looked like something out of a Dr. Seuss book. Anna wanted to call her pipe the Butter Battle Bowl, but Chloe thought that naming a glass piece was too silly and stonerish. In that moment, though, she wondered if there was ever a name too silly for something she only ever used to smoke weed.

The bowl itself was caked with resin, and smelled like it too. Chloe wondered if she needed to find a pipe cleaner right that second or if she could smoke this, go to bed, and soak the bowl in rubbing alcohol tomorrow. She sucked in; it wasn't the clearest, but it was okay. She took a few pinches of weed and sprinkled them into the bowl, grabbed a lighter, and walked back to the bed. She sat down, lit the bowl, and inhaled. No sooner did she exhale, Anna asked, "Hey, can I hit that?" as she peeled the pillow away from her eyes.

"Look who's up," Chloe said, handing Anna the bowl.

Anna took a hit from the still-burning bowl and exhaled a thin, silvery cloud of smoke that seemed to glimmer when it hit the lamplight.

"Is there any left?" asked Chloe.

"Yeah, there's another hit or two, I think." Anna handed the bowl back to Chloe.

"Thanks," replied Chloe. She lit the bowl again, inhaled, and then released a cloud of smoke from her mouth. "Did you get to sleep at all?"

"A little. I don't think I had any dreams or anything."

"Cool. I think this bowl's kicked."

Chloe handed the bowl to Anna, who put it on the porcelain plate by their bed. Chloe put her head on the pillow and started to feel the tension melting away from her neck down to her toes. She took a deep breath in, a deep breath out, and coughed.

"Hey Anna?"

"Yeah?"

"What are we really going to do when the world ends?"

"I have no fucking clue," Anna murmured.

"Well, I want us to start a horse farm out in the country somewhere, maybe West Virginia or something," explained Chloe. "We can grow pot plants and other crops and stuff, and we can learn to shoot guns. It could be a huge collective with a bunch of queers, trans girls, and two-spirit folks all living and working on the farm and taking care of the horses and each other. We'll have family dinners and skill shares and no electricity. It could really be beautiful."

"Uh huh," replied Anna. Even though she seemed to respond coherently, she was fast asleep.

Chloe stared at Anna, watching her lover's chest rise and fall with her breath. She tried to breathe in time with her, but kept losing count. She filled her head with thoughts of nuclear winter, the EMP, the slow melting of the polar icecaps, earthquakes, tsunamis, pandemics, oil spills, flash fires, and all of the atrocities that humanity was too young and innocent to even conceive of. As she looked out of the window, she watched the dark, wet night fade into the pale, dry blue of almost sunrise, savoring the deep azure shade of four in the morning. She could hear the birds start to chirp. She wished she were on a beach somewhere like Rehoboth, Asbury Park, Riis, or Rockaway. Maybe she could convince Anna to go while the weather was still nice.

The sunrise was tepid. Only a few weak strands of gold and pink seemed to reach through the clouds. The sky, the water, the world was so far from being theirs. Chloe closed her eyes and prayed for sleep.

Night of the Dead Lesbians
Bridget Liang

It's been a long month of directing Season Five of *Vampire Youth*, but we're finally done. I'm rubbing my temples to get rid of this damn headache that's been growing steadily all day. The crew is packing away and securing equipment. *I can't wait to get out of here.* Roxy is talking to me about her schedule. Something about filming on another show, and I hum and haw non-committally. Her voice is the reason why I have this damn headache in the first place. Because she's the love interest of my leading man, she's in EVERY. DAMN. EPISODE. If it wasn't for SAG-AFTRA's affirmative action policy, I wouldn't have hired her at all. Asians only make up one percent of the population; they're represented just fine as is. Why the fuck are they complaining? Being Jess Mavis, the world famous director of popular horror/teen drama, is so hard sometimes. Roxy's acting, I grudgingly admit, is spectacular, but she just doesn't *look* the part of the love interest.

Roxy follows me back to my office, and thank fuck Danny and Kevin are waiting there to hang out with me. I wave them over enthusiastically in hopes that I can use them to shake her off. I ask them about how they're going to spend their time off. Danny launches into a long-winded story about going on vacation with his newest girlfriend. Every time Roxy tries to interrupt, either Danny or Kevin, oblivious to the situation, exclaim excitedly about some inane thing like the codependent duo that they are. I smirk to myself as Roxy storms out of the studio. *Typical diva.* I turn my attention back to Kevin and ask if I can help him plot out his schedule for next season. Between directing a new show, his first movie, and convention appearances, I want to make sure I have my stars set up for the year. Both Kevin and Danny are such talented young men (albeit a little naive)—they're going somewhere great one day.

I hear on the security radio about a commotion going on at the front door and don't pay any attention. *Security will take care of it.* Kevin and Danny are now doing their best-friends, touchy-feely thing, so I reach for a bottle of scotch and settle down in my black leather sofa chair. I try to make my office comfortable and, most importantly, *masculine*. After all, I spend most of my time here. The wife is a nag. If it wasn't for the pre-nup and the kids, I would be gone. Luckily, she doesn't know about how my personal assistant *assists* me.

Suddenly and in unison, Kevin, Danny, and I jump in our seats, startled by the tinny scream coming from the radio. Kevin's eyebrows knit and he frowns, giving his co-star comforting, manly face pets. A second scream emits from the radio. It sounds like security is saying something about... zombies?

Huh. *Zombies*. Zombies were last season, when a hoard of zombies tried to take over Nosferatu Collegiate School. That was fun to film. The special effects department had a field day coming up with especially gruesome extras.

I turn over to my star actors and ask them what they think is going on. Danny thinks we should leave the building now. *Could be crazy fans that got past security*, he says. *After all, we got the highest ratings we've ever had on the show last season.*

Grabbing my Italian leather wallet and keys, I shepherd the guys out, locking the door to my office carefully. It's important that my man cave is protected. We stroll towards the back door amidst the crew packing up. Then there is shouting and creaking coming from the studio doors. This draws everyone's attention. Even Roxy has stopped her nail filing, or whatever useless diva thing she does, and is staring at the doors.

The doors rattle and shake and the radio is surprisingly silent. Danny and Kevin tug on my expensive Armani shirt (*ugh, wrinkles!*) and suggest we try to pick up the pace. *Jess, we need to move faster.* I agree with them immediately. We hastily creep towards the back door before everyone else gets a clue. The lighting guy, Fred, has the same idea. We left not a moment too soon. The studio door bursts open and a pack of screaming women rush in. (*You gotta give props to these fangirls for their skill in organizing, costuming, and makeup—all for their love of Vampire Youth.*) And then one of them bites the makeup artist, whose name I can't be bothered to remember, and she screams, which quickly turns into a groan. Fuck! Rabid fans! (*Wait, that'd make a good idea for next season.*) I imagine a group of women from the local mad house that have broken out and have insinuated themselves into the school. They'd be wearing sexy torn nurse outfits, and they'd enthrall Danny and Kevin's characters with their wily charms as they try to take over Nosferatu Collegiate.

Us four guys dash out the back door and into the hall leading to the dressing rooms. Why the fuck are we so far away from the nearest fire exit again? *No good fucking contractors who built this place.* It makes no sense at all, and the entire crew has become a stampede coming from behind us. The fanatical fangirls are also not far away either. Fuck! FUCK. They are picking off stragglers, and I dare not look back as their cries and moans echo through the narrow hallways. Somehow, Fred ends up at the back of the pack. I hear him scream as he's taken down by a fangirl.

I'm gasping for breath (*damn, I really need to work out*), and Kevin and Danny are practically carrying me. The crew and the hoard of fangirls are catching up. And yes! Freedom! We burst through the emergency doors like a trio of whales breaching the surface of the water to breathe, and I take in a deep breath of fresh, Californian smog!

The parking lot is across the outdoor sets (*FUCK*), and I don't think I'll make it at this rate. I wheeze out my realization to Danny and Kevin, who protest that we'll get out of this together. So they half carry me, half stumble with me, across the high school track field like it's *Saving Private Ryan*.

We don't get very far. I end up collapsing onto my hands and knees on the third base of the baseball diamond at the far end of the field. Kevin stumbles and starfishes on home base, followed by Danny tripping over Kevin. He lands right on his co-star's belly. I'm trying to get my breath back while breathing in dirt. By the time I've got enough oxygen in my blood to function, I see the crew scattered all over the field.

I see The Hoard bursting through the doors like that scene from *Dawn of the Dead*. (*Note to self: remember to refer to the wife's ex's kids as this the next time we host Christmas Dinner.*)

Fuck. There's something really fucking crazy going on with these girls. One looks like Lena, Hero Princess, decked out in leather with a very authentic looking boomerang belted to her waist. Lena snatches the second cameraman and bites him like he's a spare rib.

Another fangirl looks like Kara, the Wiccan priestess, from that show with the tiny brunette werewolf slayer. The stunt coordinator escapes her clutches and... he pounces on Kevin's stunt double, locking lips with him?!? *Are they really making out with each other?* What the fuck? I didn't know they were gay! I mean, it's cool, gay power and all that, but why the fuck are they making out *right now?*

Fangirl that looks like Poisson from that lesbian penitentiary show is shambling away from two extras who are... fucking?!?! *Why are there suddenly so many fags in my crew?*

One of the fangirls spot us, and that's good enough motivation for me to run again! I pull Danny and Kevin to their feet and we're speeding towards the parking lot again. The momentary rest we had really wasn't enough. (*Hey, I'm a busy man producing a number of highly rated shows. I don't have the time to get back the abs I had in college.*)

We pass by a lot of the crew fucking or doing tantric yoga poses or... something. I don't care. I don't understand. I don't want to know. I don't want to look. But I do notice the hairstylist and set designer scissoring and fucking. Mmmm, I wish I could stop and watch those two go at it!

Lawn gives way to pavement. Yes! We finally reached the parking lot! Kevin and Danny separate from me to look for their cars. I automatically go for my Camaro but it's not there. OH FUCK. I forgot that I took the wife's minivan today. I fumble around for the right key. Just when I find them, I drop them.

Bright hot pain blooms from my right shoulder. I may be into biting, but usually I'm the one doing the biting. I yell (*well, manly screaming*) and turn around. It's the girl who played Emilee, a disposable lesbian minor character who was on Season Three of *Vampire Youth*. On the show, she was out on a date with her girlfriend, Katie, and Danny was also there flirting with them when the leader of the witch coven, the big bad of the season, abducted Emilee to be a virgin sacrifice for a love potion to get Danny to marry her. And this fangirl... No... *She's a fucking zombie! A real fucking zombie!* She's cackling over me, gloating about something, and says all this stuff about revenge that I don't care about because... all I can look at is Danny and

Kevin! They're huddled together screaming by Danny's car as a couple of zombies pass by them for some reason. I am entranced by the pale length and brown moles of Danny's neck that I want my mouth all over. Fuck. What... what's happening to me? Why am I suddenly thinking gay thoughts? I'm not gay!

Emilee screeches something to the other lesbian zombies. I think I hear phrases like "lesbian book club," "healing circle," "vegan/gluten free food," and "in the U-Haul." I distinctly hear her say that their job was done here. The lesbian zombies are all hollering, hooting, and cheering as they run off studio property and into the sunset.

After the last of them leave, soft moans break the silence behind me. I turn around and am blown away by what's now in front of me.

Danny's lips are wrapped around Kevin's cock and, fuck, *I want that.* I want that to be me or have that done to me—I don't care. All thoughts of the personal assistant are gone as my eyes glue to Danny's pink, hollowed lips around that fat cock. He's also lifting up Kevin's shirt. *Damn,* I think while smacking my lips. *I never appreciated Kevin's abs until now.*

Kevin turns to me. I never noticed how warm and sensual his brown eyes were until right now.

"Jess Mavis!" he yells at me. "Get over here and fuck one of us!"

I stumble over to him and comply. Huh. Neither of them have been bitten. Were they secretly gay lovers this whole time? Kevin pulls down the zipper to my slacks. *I am getting so hard.* Then I black out.

I wake up, sandwiched between two warm bodies. I smell sex, sweat, cum, and ass, and I've never been so content. Danny mewls in his sleep in front of me and Kevin casually caresses my belly. My ass is sore, but it is a good kind of sore. Maybe those lesbian zombies were a blessing in disguise. HA! (*So much for their revenge.*) I chuckle to myself and think about inviting these two over to my office more often for "bonding time" and "character development." Personal assistant? I could care less about her. The wife never needs to know about this either.

"Sir! Jess! There's another zombie coming this way," the audio engineer screams out of nowhere. The man is covered in love bites, which I wish I had given him.

"The zombies are alright. Their bites make you gay, I'm cool... Maybe you'd like to join us?" I implore and lick my lips suggestively.

"But sir, she's covered in blood!"

I swear and look up from my pile of warmth. On a warpath heading for us is this tranny minor vampire villain from Season One whose name, I recall, is Stiles. I remember the shot where she was brutally killed. The cinematography won me an award for best shot in a new TV show. And Stiles was covered in blood—just like she is now.

She reaches us surprisingly quickly and lifts me up by the hair (*owwww!*). Her face is contorted with rage, and that's definitely real blood on her lips. Blood oozes onto my neck as she gets closer to my ear. The last thing I hear is her growling, and these final four words:

"Jess Mavis is not a gift."

Goldilocks Lynched

Lawrence Walker III

Here's how the story begins, ends, and lives. You have heard the story told of Goldilocks and the Three Bears. Goldilocks not only stole the porridge, chairs, and beds, but her continuous taking continued as she stole and stole: stole everything. There were no bears; there was us, our people, all other brown people.

Mother and Father, there's a vast separation of time that pulls like rope: me away from you.

Each tiny bristle on the rope signifies; each breaking year yanks. Goldilocks and her counterpart were the creators of this rope. In fact, they were the ones pulling it. You could see the white smudges pressed down on the bristles like a paintbrush. Goldilocks sat in fear of her counterpart, who stood in the shadows with a wig and a striped top hat, sticking out its pallid finger at her with entitlement. Goldilocks saw that it had a body and mind of its own.

Goldilocks was indifferent towards all at the other end of the rope she held, where our brown and Black ancestors stood tied. She wanted to cull every inch of the rope and pull every bristle for herself: to use her silhouette to enchain all the brown and Black bodies that stood down the rope, all of us. In order to take up all our space, Goldilocks ran up each pedestal and each stair to claim us all at once: the pallid silhouette a standard. There was a hierarchy that spanned between us and the shadowed, screeching figure who smelled of wet dog hair and patchouli.

Goldilocks and her counterpart were superior. They knew this. They held the rope; they held each pedestal; they stole indigenous land. The silhouette remained transparent in the air. It found its way into us.

Over time, it took its new form in locks, padded cells, bullets, lynching, suicide: red, white, and blue. It took its form to destroy the inner root of our skin, where our foundation—our defiance—were suppressed. Suppression associated with death; associated with compliance; associated with the problem. Associated with our beauty becoming vile, dreadful, wretched, useless.

Out of Goldilocks' shadow her counterpart revealed its face. What an ugly being it was: eyes of a colonizer, wrinkled skin of fragility, entitled boney fingers. In its hands it held lead and an eraser. It scrubbed against all of our fallen ancestor's names, bodies, sexualities, disabilities, culture, reason: our fluidity of gender and our bodies that were absent of gender. It opened its crusty, chapped lips and yelled, "Paint it white, all of it!"

Goldilocks nodded in agreement as she sat on the same hierarchical pedestal. They erased, erased, and erased.

Uncle Sam was Goldilocks's counterpart's name. He held this lead in his hands, wrote his ideas of who held rights, who felt struggle, who wasn't erased. Goldilocks knew never to trust Uncle Sam, who admired her beauty foremost with envy, and who abused her with his looks and with his yelling. But still, Goldilocks remembered, her relationship with Uncle Sam helped her. Goldilocks thought of herself first, remaining on the pedestal, forgetting and erasing, forgetting and erasing.

In front of Goldilocks and Uncle Sam, guarding them and pacing back and forth, was a person that looked alike to us. It was one of our own, draped in garments that told stories of the pallid light case upon them by Goldilocks and Uncle Sam. You see it in their face and in each heavy breath you could hear: "Masta', masta', I serve for you," "Masta' I kill for you," "I remain complacent for you masta'," in every step they took. "Wait a minute you see this badge master I pledge for you. No one can come up to this pedestal I hold for you. It is held in only regard to upholding you masta'." "Whoa, you smell that, masta', it's underneath here. It's the death of my own damn people, well niggas should've known not to be too loud, belligerent jiggaboos, against your order masta'. Against our order. I hold no remorse. Welp we'll sweep them up anyway, don't give a damn about them anyway, just trophies for my collection. I will provide social control and protect all your property, masta'."

Before the Coon could speak any more, our people got really disruptive, feeling a want to be ungovernable: the feeling of not wanting to be silenced anymore. Not only by Goldilocks and Uncle Sam, as we knew and expected their harm, but to see one of our own kind doing the work more effectively than this pallid whiteness made us unruly, clamorous in our rage.

"Fuck you, Coon." Objects began to fly at the coon, aiming for his throat, so he would never come back to add our people's bodies underneath the pedestals he defended.

He turned to us, surrounded with the pallor like white flames, "Why are you all so damn angry, nun uh, that is not going to happen today. Your questioning, your demands, and your violent ways of going about it is not going to work. We are going to have to put that to rest now. Masta' is not going to like this at all."

Everyone screamed. Echoing each other's pain, we yelled, "Don't you get it, Coon? We are fighting for you, too; why must you stab us harder through our backs? Why must you stomp on our faces while reaching out your hand? Masta' doesn't care about you; don't you believe you deserve—"

Cutting off the crowd of our people, "Criminals! You say I'm doing the work of masta'? I'm the true model of good negro niggas; you are the white ones. I represent you god dammit, there is no other way than my way. Prepare to die, as I am here to brutalize, and uphold my and masta's needs."

Here the Coon pulled out his gun as the finishing point, wanting to make sure they would measure our souls by each tool of brutalization from the whiteness. Before they caressed their hands around the trigger, before they took their next life-sucking breath, slit went their neck, as our bodies swarmed to rip apart every piece of the Coon. We felt hurt and wanted our pain to be heard: to make sure that the whiteness that existed was no more. "Death to the Coon! Death to the Coon! Death to the Coon!" "Off with the heads of Goldilocks and Uncle Sam! You are next."

Under the pedestal sat our ancestors, sat us, constantly asking, "What about us? What about our existences? You two can't experience what we experience on those horrid pedestals made of our backs, your pallid glow, and your pallid silhouettes."

We yelled, "We don't want the pedestals; we don't want the superior glow that holds you over us."

We, Black people demanded, "Stop erasing our struggles, our culture, our existences, and every foundational thing we stand for. Our resources you exploit; our bodies you latch through bondage. The inaccessibility you create, the bullets you shoot us with, the rope you cut and hung us with, the padded bars you lock us up with, the suppression you ingrain in our bodies: the whole system designed to eat our insides out."

We yelled tenderly, sobbing, water-eyed, "We are tired of your pallid existences; we are tired of your colonizing, Uncle Sam, and your colonizing, Goldilocks. We are fed up. We are ready to take the rope you built, the weapons you used against us, the suppression, the bullets you shot, the anger, and reclaim it. To take down the pedestal you sit on, and the pallid silhouette that holds you up."

Uncle Sam started cowardly blurting, whipping, and abrasively yelling to our Black ancestors, "Niggers. Tar babies. All of you tar babies, you think you have it hard, what about me? For I am the one who is colonized first. Why don't you understand that, I can't do everything. I can't do anything! Why do you complain so much? Why don't you work your way up the stairs, up to the pedestal where Goldilocks and I stand? Don't you see how these rights I've written apply to you? Don't you see the systems I set in place for you? Don't you want to die in these systems? Don't you want to be stripped of all of your identities? Don't you wanna die? What are you all anyway? Useless. Disposable. Tools. Eraser shavings. Hush! You peasants hush."

Our Black ancestors broke out in song. We cried out in resistance. We consented to collective protection.

We brought in a rope found out by the sea. Barnacles of silky melanin slithered on the surface. Those who touched it fell. The victims fell to it, such as Emmett Till, every Black woman hung, every fallen Black trans woman and trans-femme person used as a prized trophy from our people: we who did not get the same sense of urgency from our people when our bodies hung like rotten berries. We clung to ourselves as Uncle Sam and Goldilocks sat in silence, or cheered our death from on top of their pedestal.

We joined in with the brown folks to get a more complete, formidable strength to tie Uncle Sam from his throat down. We threw the rope full force, with every spiritual ancestor on both sides guiding the rope to its rightful destination. Just like the clanks that locked up our wrists: labeled us slaves, criminals, devils, super predators, men in dresses, unreasonable, angry Black women, jezebels, enemies of the state and niggers. Incapable of feeling, of living, of love: unable to be sentient. The rope locked, tightened, and closed with a breeze, and the colonizer eyes that once were in the socket of Uncle Sam were no more. His striped hat crashed down to the ground. Everything our Black ancestors put into the pedestal died; the pallid silhouette that held Uncle Sam superior and alive was diminished.

The crowd chanted, danced. We were shocked and took care of ourselves emotionally, as so much emotion and tears powered the pulling of the rope: powered death to the whiteness that made Uncle Sam so bright, so powerful. The whiteness was now soaked in blood: blood that symbolized all the brown and Black lives it absorbed, bombed, chewed and spat back out.

The blood still covered Goldilocks' hands, hair, skin. Goldilocks knew she was next. Her pallid silhouette still alive: oppressing with its light.

Goldilocks began to think up a way to keep her neck from being compressed next. Our Black ancestors yelled, "Goldilocks, we repeat, we come to take back everything we built, everything you stole: the pallid silhouette that holds you superior to us and discredits our struggle with yours, that holds your beauty, original; your beauty, the only way to obtain. We come in vindication to all the oppression your pallid light has had on us. We mourn; we hold our heads in faith, sobbing, tenderly, flooded with anger, on the edge of ourselves. Take that eraser you hold in your hands and break it. Break the pedestal you are clinging to. Recognize that pallid glow that makes you superior. If you do not we will pull you down by the same rope you designed, and we will be ungovernable."

Sweat trickled down. Drip, drip, drip, like it never did before, on Goldilocks face. There was no way for her to run now: no beds or porridge to hide away in. Quickly, Goldilocks responded, pandering to our people in anger, in fear, in envy, in guilt: to lie and continue to follow in the same final footsteps Uncle Sam took.

Goldilocks yelled to all down below,

"Well I'll be damn, you niggas up to no good. You've got it all wrong. Who do you think you are talking to!? Who do you think I am!? I can't have any compromises without you making a ruckus. I'm dearly afraid of you all. I'm afraid of your voice, your beauty. My god do you look bright when you're empowered, when you're not dehumanized, when you're not drowned in your self-hate, when you challenge me. How frightening!

Yet, I'm merely doing my part. I could never perpetuate this pallid light, this pallid silhouette you speak of.

I faced abuse from Uncle Sam. I experience pain too; screw that pain you speak of down there you cretins! You think we don't stand on the same side?"

As she said this her pallid light was vibrant and bright as the rays of a son.

"I am the one you thank for your liberation, as I included you. Yeah, yeah, I pushed you to the back, I discredited you, I stripped your identity, but that is freedom. That is the freedom you deserve. Who was the one there to teach you your language? Who was the one there to acquaint you with your chains and bondage?

Who was the one there to devalue all the work you did up there? Who was the one there to give you your rights to vote? I sent you death, I mean freedom. I enchained your minds; I included you, alright. You get nothing, you get nothing, you unappreciative niggas: all you tar babies.

Did I not stand side by side with you? Is this all what you wanted? Educate me, god dammit. I demand you educate me, and cater your feelings to me this instant!"

This was the last ever heard from Goldilocks, as the Black and brown people in unison nodded their agreement to tug the rope with all their might. Our people yelled emphatically,

"Goldilocks, everything has been said and done. You could never grant us freedom, as we have taken our liberation in our hands. Liberation we will die for. You erased us from your idea of liberation, gave us the idea of freedom to chew on. You erased us, you demonized us, you killed us with every inch of space you took up on your pedestal.

Every inch of space your pallid silhouette took from our struggle. You contributed to the oppression we feel, but the moment we pull this rope, there will be no oppression any more. There will be no more erasure. There will be none of your pallid glow on our bodies. We will live, as we are gifted, as we are the foundation to everything you and Uncle Sam took. We pull this in remembrance of the countless deaths that fell to your pallid silhouette. We pull this rope for our future children, who live for themselves: liberated, young at heart and Black!"

Alike to the pulling of a curtain, the blinds were lifted and the rope was tied. The colonizer air shot out of Goldilocks' sternum as she was hung. People yelled, "Goldilocks Lynched!!" "Uncle Sam lynched!!"

The pallid light deceased, and everything faded to black... faded to brown. It read Blackness and brownness. We live in our ancestors, and our ancestors live in us.

Sincerely, Love,
Hootie

An Essay About Being a Non Male/Non Female Person in the Literary World, Written in the Form of a Dream

Moss Angel

You are on a beach. The beach is beautiful, with bright orange sand and an olive green ocean lapping against the shore. The whole sky is pink. You feel like the world has been color-shifted, but you can't remember the "right" colors. Your sense of self has changed, but you do not know this yet.

You walk along the beach until you come upon a small beach village. You are very hungry. This village is full of people, and the people in it have a particular way of doing things.

You wander into a crowded building. There are two tables, and at these tables are mountains of food. It is a buffet. You attempt to join one of the lines until someone comes up to you and says this line is for people who have only a left arm, and the amount of food you get will be determined by how strong that arm is. You look down and see you have three arms. They are soft and supple, but do not bulge with muscle.

You try to enter second line. This line's pile of food is half the size of the pile on the first table, but is still significant. In this line you are told that you must have only a right arm, and that the food will be given out depending on how soft and supple that arm is. You point out that you do have a right arm and that it is very supple. They point out that you also have two other arms and direct you to a third table. This table is in a separate building. This building isn't a building so much as it is a tent. The pile of food is tiny.

You enter the line and you are told that you must have an arm growing from the middle of your chest. Your third arm is growing from the middle of your back. They tell you that the people in the other building are most impressed by those who have an arm growing from the middle of their chest. You say you do not have this and how can you get food.

They hand you a dull knife from the cupboard and a needle and thread and tell you that you could always move your third arm to the middle of your chest. They tell you that if you really wanted to, you could also cut off your other two arms, as that would most impress the people in the other building and get you the most food. You are told that the people in the other building are very entertained by single arms growing from the middle of a person's chest, but that extraneous limbs are too much. You are told that it is politically important right now for people who are in the other building to make sense of people who don't have a big, muscular left arm or a soft, supple right arm, but instead have an arm growing directly from the middle of their chest. You are told that most of the people in the line at this tent have only a single arm growing from the middle of their chest and that is why it is important right now for that to be the focus, so we can get the people in the building to love and accept us and give us more food.

You notice that while it is true that most of the people in this line have a single arm growing from the middle of their chest, that most of these limbs have scars at the base. Some of them are gangrenous and some of them are bleeding to death.

You are told that you cannot enter the line for now but if you would like you can enter the courtyard and dance to impress the people from the other building while they dine. That they might give you some of their food if you impress them enough.

You enter the courtyard and see some dying people who have tried very hard to make their bodies impress the people from the other building while they dance. They are barely receiving any food at all from the people from the first building. You dance for a little bit but soon get frustrated and angry. You hate these people.

You go to an abandoned corner of the courtyard and you cut off all your arms. It is incredibly painful. You leave them there on the ground and you begin to dance. Blood is pouring and spattering all around you as you dance. You dance closest to the people from the first line in the other building and you get blood all over them and their precious food. You spin and dance wildly and blood covers their faces. They are not amused. You begin to get food from the other dancers, especially from the most gangrenous and unhappy of them. It isn't much but it rejuvenates your strength. You dance into the first building. You spin and bleed all over the food of the people in this building. You contaminate their whole food supply. They send their strongest left-arm-havers to stop you, but you know you have already ruined their food. As they approach, you fall down, weak from blood loss. You die happy.

Broke Pieces
AR Mannylee Rushet

I feel it in my throat
the way you ignore me.
If only I could separate my head from my body
the way that you can.

Talk about your elbow
as though it is easy to separate your elbow from your shoulder.

My emotion feels unexplained and like a sucker punch to you,
tearing through the sky sheets of your white world.
Within reason only because you don't understand the equation
its history.

This misunderstanding feels like blood has
slipped through my fingers.
I can't bring to tune the song of violence, its melody.
I don't know how to discuss what violence is with you.

So slanted are the hills you've been playing on for so long,
I'd probably just fall down and scrape my knees.
And my knees have been scraped again and again;
at this point I don't really care who cut them.

Or for the lily tenderness of professed innocence.

All I know is that they stood by and without the music of their box,
watched me bleed and then professed themselves innocent.

To look at the innocence of a person and think
that their pieces are all the same
is to have given them broken pieces
ones that you know they can't possibly defend with.

So even when valiant, their weapon might as well be invisible.

It is you who gave them the thing they must somberly wield:
the mirage of their blows against the wind,
hoping just to prick your vile, thick skin.

GAUNT
Luna Merbruja

She was not herself after that night. We were lying on the roof of my sky blue mini-SUV. I was on my belly trying to avert the intense vertigo I experience when gazing into huge open spaces, and she was on her back staring intently at the twinkling void.

"Ooh, a shooting star!" She gave my hand a firm squeeze. "And ooh! There's Sagittarius's bow and arrow!"

She tugged on my arm, and I lifted my head up to follow her pointed finger to no avail. The stars spun after a few seconds of trying to focus. I grunted an affirmative sound, feeling a pang of guilt for lying, before facing away again.

"There's another star that's moving really slowly," she trailed off, her hand gripping mine tight.

"Are you okay?" I turned my head to face her and caught her petrified look. "Hey, is something wrong?"

She didn't blink. The darkness around us sang with crickets and the distant shuffling of nocturnal creatures.

"This star is... moving," she said slowly. "It's not a plane, because all the planes I've seen have red flashing lights, and you can hear them... and shooting stars don't last this long across the sky."

I studied her face and noticed tears beginning to form at the corners of her eyes. She remained motionless.

I retreated into my head to remain calm. The darkness offered no comfort. It seemed like every insect was rallying a war cry, and then we flinched as a bat flew swiftly above our heads. When I looked back at her, she was still staring, streams of silent tears glistening through the dark.

I thought she would come back to me. But what came back was something else entirely.

"I would prefer that you don't enter my room anymore," she says as she pours herself a third cup of coffee. "I need my privacy to be respected. Do you understand?" She hunches across the room without once meeting my eyes.

"I'm sorry, I won't bother you again." I reach out to hug her, but she dodges me and ducks back into her room. I stare at the closed bedroom door, straining to hear any clue that might reveal what's going on.

It's been a month since that night and we haven't slept in the same bed since. She goes to work with empty eyes and comes home with an emptier hunger. I can't get her to eat or have a conversation with me.

I don't know what to do.

"I know I'm not supposed to go through her things, but I was so fucking scared. I panicked and just wanted answers." I pick under my fingernails, avoiding my therapist's eyes, feeling like a child who's been caught sneaking cookies.

"What did you find?" Her voice is even, non-judgmental. It's exactly what I need.

"A bunch of weird alien shit... like, extraterrestrials. There's all these books with highlighting and sticky notes. I don't—I don't know what to make of it all." I cover my face with my hands, ashamed of the tears swelling in my eyes. My therapist waits a moment for me to take a few deep breaths to gather myself.

"Why is she researching aliens?" She leans forward with furrowed eyebrows.

"Remember that night I told you about? I think she thinks she saw something. I mean, there's no way for me to know for sure because she won't talk to me."

The loneliness suddenly seizes me and I burst into tears. My therapist crosses the room and offers me a tissue. It's the smallest kindness I haven't received in weeks, and it rips me open raw.

It took a few months to establish a new rhythm. I stopped trying to intervene in her "research" and she has stopped verbally speaking to me altogether. She pays her bills on time and only responds to emails related to house necessities.

She has new quirks too. Before, she used to leave lipstick stains on every mug that met her lips. Now, she only uses a single cup for coffee and no other dish.

She doesn't turn on lights anymore. Sometimes I'm shocked by her sudden appearance in the kitchen or exit from the bathroom. She used to laugh in these moments, but now she simply glides by without a breath.

Her body shows signs of her retreat, from the way her belly has crawled up behind her bones and her eye sockets deepened to hollow voids. Her thick curly hair is now limp, her mahogany skin now bleached sand.

My lover is a ghost, our bed a tombstone, and her room the great unknown.

I shouldn't do this, but I cannot take it anymore. I'm waiting for her in her room, sitting on the edge of the couch, flipping through a manila folder filled with blurry photos of supposed extraterrestrials.

I had done a bit of my own research. I want to understand, to connect. I am feeling... desperate. *Lonely.* I wish I could return us to a year ago when we took a week off to visit Yellowstone. When we held hands and had long staring contests while sitting on broad rocks in the middle of mild rivers.

My reminiscing is cut short by her abrupt entrance into the room. Immediately, her face brightens with rage.

"What the fuck?! I TOLD you to stay out of my room!"

Instead of panic, I feel relief at the emotional outburst. I stay quiet and still.

"You don't know what you've just done," she says.

"You're right, I don't know! Please tell me something, *anything.*"

"They're coming for you next." Her voice is steady, almost smug. I study her for a second and notice a pattern of inch-long lines of red across her forearms, chest, and neck.

"What... what happened to you?" I stand up and reach towards her, but she steps back from me. I grab her hand and feel a powerful shock emanate from the skin I touched.

"What the fuck was that?!"

"My defense system. I guess it's time to try it out."

She reaches behind her neck and emits a sickly clicking sound. Instantly, her eyes cloud with crimson. The slits across her body ooze a mercury-like substance that hardens into thick plates. Her jaw unhinges, revealing a second mandible with three rows of canines. Her ribs crack wide open, except her skin doesn't tear. A third slick appendage emerges out from her belly button.

I cower backwards, tripping on the couch and falling to the ground. I shut my eyes tight, hearing her body snap back into shape with one loud *crack*. My heart is beating through my throat. I pray to God that this is simply a nightmare.

The air in the room thickens with a ghastly scent. As I hyperventilate, I begin to feel lightheaded. I feel a needle-sharp prick into the back of my neck that numbs my entire body. I can't move, nor open my eyes, but I remain cognizant. I can hear the sounds of my bones crunching. I can feel the pressure of a heavy, hot wetness encasing my body.

The last thing I hear is a victorious cackle, and the sound of a booming plane arriving on the roof of the house.

God Empress Susanna
A.K. Blue

Susanna waited for the bus in the cold November drizzle, her lower half coiled on the ground, the rest upright, bus pass in her mouth. Being exothermic, she had to struggle against cold-induced fatigue. She longed to be back in bed, burrowing under the covers, then recollected with irony all the times she had felt that way back when she could drive to work, back when she had body heat, back when she was human. It reminded her that things could always be worse.

Susanna hated being seen, and here she was on display to an endless procession of people, the slow, heavy morning commuter traffic on the two-lane road. Once in a while a car would honk or someone would yell something out the window. She wanted to crawl into the bare trees and wet leaves behind her but had to stay in the exact right spot or the automated bus wouldn't register her as a potential passenger. The spot was marked by a rusty manhole cover set into the ground among dead weeds and litter.

She had worried that she would miss the bus, stuck on the other side of the road where the apartment complex was, waiting for a break in the traffic so she could crawl across, dreading the sight of the bus's familiar pattern of lights emerging from the grey mist. But the bus was late. Periodically a heavy drop fell on her from the power lines overhead.

She shook herself awake when the bus finally appeared. She inched forward as it slowed, brakes gasping, warning lights blinking. The door folded sideways, and she wiggled up the steps and held the bus pass up to the scanner until it beeped.

It was warm inside, and she spotted an empty seat near the back. She undulated down the aisle, teetering but not falling when the bus jolted forward. Feet moved out of her way, but otherwise the passengers ignored her. Even so, she felt conspicuous. She crawled onto the seat and carefully dropped the pass into the blue nylon bag belted around her midsection.

She gazed out the fogged-up window, afraid if she looked around the bus she would find someone staring at her. Everything looked desolate in the grey light. As the bus made its way into town, the trees and driveways became rows of houses, then streets full of buildings. All too soon, the bus arrived at the mall. She slithered out onto the pavement and towards the row of glass doors.

The mall was empty. No music played, no water jetted from the imitation marble basin at the center of the food court. Nothing opened until ten. Voices and metallic clangs echoed in the bright, cavernous spaces as Susanna hurried through, bunching up and stretching out like a giant inchworm. The store where she worked, Happyworld, was all the way at the other end of the mall, beyond Shop Rite and the second-run multiplex, one of the two anchor stores.

Happyworld's doors were locked until it opened, so she pushed the buzzer and waited. Bill, the manager, appeared. He was a short, stocky man with a shaved head, moving with a quick, irritated stride. He unlocked the door and held it open.

"Hello, Susanna," he said without enthusiasm.

She followed him across the store, past row after row of video games, sports equipment, small robots, toys, books, digital instruments, phones, to the customer service desk where the other employees stood. Fluorescent tubes among the ducts and wires up on the high ceiling cast a shadowless light.

"Okay, we're all here," Bill said, picking up his clipboard. "Cindy, you're at the cash register. Mike, Jim, Tracy, you're on the floor. Today is a truck day, so I need the rest of you in the back room."

Susanna had drawn herself down so that she peeped over the edge of the counter at the others. There wasn't much work she could do. She was a liability, costing the other employees money. She was only supposed to have been an earthworm long enough to use its ability to change gender, so she'd have a female body when the gene therapy converted her back into human. But the latest round of spending cuts had eliminated the program while she was still a worm. As compensation, they'd passed a job protection bill so those trapped in worm form couldn't be fired.

"I don't need to tell you we're not doing well," Bill continued. "We need to sell more Happycard memberships. That's the key to building a customer base. I don't want any customers walking out of here without a Happycard. Okay, let's get going."

As Susanna wriggled towards the back room, she detoured through the book section, passing the science fiction shelves. There it was, the canon, all six volumes, rearranged by her in sequential instead of alphabetical order, from *Dune* to *Chapterhouse Dune*. She had obsessed over them since becoming a worm, rereading them over and over. Right now she was in the middle of *God Emperor of Dune*. She loved to imagine being a titanic sandworm powering her way through the solid earth, mouth glowing like a furnace, crystal teeth glittering like diamonds.

Cold air flooded the backroom, pouring in from the open garage door in the truck bay. Susanna wilted. The drivers were still unloading, stacking cardboard boxes from the back of the truck. Stu, who supervised the back room, a wiry, sharp-featured man who told deadpan, violent stories from when he had been an alcoholic, said, "I'm going to take a cigarette break. You guys hang out 'til I get back." Susanna curled up in a corner, trying to minimize her surface area. She closed her eyes.

An alien sun blazed in the eternally cloudless sky. Hot winds stirred. People from all over Arrakis, wearing the decorative masks and illustrated robes of Festival, lined the road, hoping to get a glimpse of their ruler, the galaxy's ruler, the great worm herself, Susanna. Wherever she glanced, the people cheered, jumped, danced, excited by her notice.

An attack could come at any time, *she thought, conscious of the security forces jogging to keep pace with the Imperial Worm Cart that carried her giant body. Every moment is a test.*

A chairdog, who must have broken out of its house to see her, pushed through the crowd, eyes wild with adoration. It tried to run alongside her, vestigial legs struggling to propel its awkward bulk, but it collapsed.

It is a projection they worship!

She focused inward, planning the many meetings that would take place when she arrived at her citadel. She had leverage over all the factions of the galaxy due to her monopoly on melange, the spice, the drug that made star travel and higher consciousness possible, but it had to be applied delicately, strategically. Impatient, she accelerated the cart, an Ixian machine that responded to her mental commands.

Stu's voice said, "Anytime you're ready, Susanna."

Susanna started. The garage door was closed, the others busy with the boxes. Embarrassed at being caught daydreaming, she crawled over to join them. If she had real worm senses she would have felt the vibrations of Stu's approach. But her human brain and nervous system could not have made sense of them. Instead, the earthworm DNA had, like a genetic algorithm, adapted her human senses to her new body. She had eyes, earholes, nostrils for smelling, taste buds. She tasted metal as she picked up a boxcutter with her mouth and bent over a box to slice it open.

It felt good to be useful for a change. "Attaboy Susanna!" Bobby said encouragingly. Bobby was a burly, friendly college-age guy who usually worked in the electronics section. Bobby was opening boxes too, and by the time Susanna had opened three Bobby had opened the rest.

"I guess there's nothing else you can do around here," Stu said. "You might as well wait in the break room so you don't get in the way."

Susanna crawled back across the store, using the shelves and aisles to hide from customers. She passed the checkout counter where Cindy, a student at the local community college, toyed with her phone. Susanna forced herself not to look. Cindy already thought she was a creep. Cis women did that, assumed you were looking at them with a sexual gaze.

Susanna wondered how much of Cindy's attractiveness was innate. She was as thin as a model, her bleached hair hung around her face, and what of her face you could see was mostly perfect white teeth and long black eyelashes. Her clothes were inexpensive but well put together. Susanna might be able to do a lot of that herself once she had a human body, if she ever did. But the thought never stopped the painful longing the sight of Cindy made her feel.

Nobody was in the break room. Susanna hid under the formica table, metal folding chairs scraping the floor as she pushed them aside. The other employees got irritated if they saw her doing nothing while they were working. She settled down.

Susanna had positioned the Imperial Worm Cart in her audience cham-

ber, *a vast bubble of air within her stone citadel. Moneo, her majordomo, was briefing her on the first meeting of the day.*

"It all comes down to melange, as usual," Moneo said. "The Bene Gesserit sisterhood wants more for their rituals."

Susanna made no response. They use their religion to control the populace, and I use the spice to control them. *She thought of the giant vault of it far below them, hidden at the center of a maze of tunnels she had burrowed herself. Sometimes she went down and swam in it, leaping about, filled with happiness.*

"I suggest we demand greater intelligence cooperation against Ix," Moneo said. "Ix has long sought to synthesize melange."

"At the prompting of the Bene Gesserit, no doubt. Yes, we will do that. It will turn them against each other, sparing us an open display of force. Ix is too valuable to be destroyed."

"Unless they synthesize the spice."

"Unless they synthesize the spice," Susanna agreed. "So we must prevent that." She paused. "This will be a subtle and difficult meeting. I must prepare myself."

I must use the spice!

She directed a thought at her cart. In response, a small, delicate machine emerged from a hatch and chopped lines of melange. The smell of cinnamon engulfed her. The tiny crystals, a pale mineral orange, sparkled as they caught the light of the drifting glowglobes. Rapt, she bent over and snorted them up with a loud whoosh.

Immediately, her awareness rippled outwards. No longer limited by her senses, she perceived her surroundings directly as pure form, crystalline objects vibrant with their energized molecules. She recognized Moneo, the guards in the hallways, the Bene Gesserit priestesses sitting in the anteroom, poised but inwardly tense.

It is an unfolding.

As the spice rush continued, the range of the crystal forms expanded, taking in the structure of the citadel, the city around it, the planet, the solar system. Everywhere in her awareness, the forms interacted, meshing like crystal gears, a direct vision of causality. She was connected to everything, no longer alone but part of a larger whole. She felt strong, serene, an unmovable mover.

Moneo, who had the blue eyes of an addict, said, "May I partake, my lady?"

"*Of course.*" *The subsection of the cart's surface with the spice server lifted, becoming a tray hovering on suspensors, and floated down to Moneo. He stooped over it with a rolled-up imperial note.*

The stars became visible through the walls of her citadel. Soon she could see stars through the floor, through the entire planet. So the guild navigators watch the stars as their ships traverse the galaxy. *The walls faded into the black of space.*

With a mental command she adjusted the glowglobes to ultraviolet. The light in the chamber became a dim, rich purple. The bright paintings of scenes from her life that ringed the chamber fluoresced, flaming against the stars like the signs of a zodiac.

Moneo looked around, cringed. No, he had only cringed mentally. She was reading his thoughts. He could see the stars too, and they overwhelmed him.

Humans! *They could not imagine the immensity of space. When they tried, they only shrank the universe into something small enough for their imaginations to contain. They shrank with it, then marvelled at how small they had become, marvelled at how they, their entire world, were insignificant motes of dust amidst the vastness of the cosmos. Insignificant motes of dust! They, large animals, the planet they were on, a massive celestial object, insignificant motes of dust! Only in their limited minds. The universe did not make Susanna feel small. She only perceived its largeness in its true dimensions.*

Even I make them feel small!

The spice server clicked back into place, retracted. She was ready.

"Summon the witches!"

The Bene Gesserit priestesses entered the chamber and glided towards the cart. No doubt they could tell she was high, but that worked to her advantage, tempting them all the more. They stopped the prescribed ten paces away.

Moneo, standing at attention, said, "Lady Susanna, God Empress of the known universe!"

"Greetings, my lady," *said Reverend Mother Anteac, the leader of the delegation.* "We have much to discuss."

Susanna studied their faces. They were practiced at concealing their thoughts. Only traces glimmered behind their controlled expressions.

But the spice hasn't peaked yet!

"Very much and very little." It was all about one thing, the spice.

Anteac showed no reaction. *"We know of your interest in Ix."*

"Technology is a force that shapes everything else. Just like religion."

"Just like you, my lady."

Then it happened. Their facial masks gave way to clarity. She could read their minds.

All their thoughts, all their plans and expectations, crystalized before her. She could see herself through their eyes, hear herself though their ears. She shared their reactions in real time. She could create exactly the effect she wanted, control the conversation to achieve her goals.

She would always say the right thing, she thought wistfully. She would know if there was anything wrong with how she looked or acted and correct it. She could be exactly who she wanted to be, living the life she wanted to live.

High heels clicked on the break room floor. Susanna recognized Cindy's confident stride. A locker door opened, and paper and plastic crackled. A chair scraped, and Cindy sat down to eat lunch.

Susanna froze. Cindy hadn't noticed her hiding under the table. She could wait until Cindy left and avoid her completely. She couldn't take Cindy's hostility right now.

Cindy munched her salad and flipped the pages of one of the old magazines on the table.

Susanna glimpsed sneakers entering the room. "Oh! Hi, Bobby!" Cindy said.

"Hey, Cindy." Coins rattled in the soda machine, machinery whirred, and a can clunked down.

"Oh god, I can't believe I ate that milkshake. I must have gained ten pounds."

"You look great to me. Come here..."

This was going wrong. Susanna hadn't meant to spy on Cindy, only to avoid her, and now the situation was getting worse with every smooch and giggle. Perhaps if she kept still Cindy and Bobby would leave without discovering her, but sitting here listening to them just felt too wrong. She had to let them know she was here, whatever the consequences. She rammed one of the table's legs so that the whole table jumped.

"Ewww! Susanna!" Cindy yelled. "She was here all the time! That's *it!*" She stood up and marched out of the room.

Susanna peeked over the tabletop. Bobby stood by the whiteboard sipping his Coke. "I didn't see anything," he said mildly.

Susanna waited, apprehensive.

Bill leaned through the door. "Susanna. We need to find something for you to do. Follow me."

She followed him out to the center of the store, where he looked around with quick jerks of his head, fingers dancing under his chin as he thought. In the aisles, the crew from the back room pushed metal carts full of the new merchandise. "It looks like they're done with the truck," he said. "I'll tell you what. You can clean up the back room."

In the back room, Stu sat alone in front of the computer. The cardboard boxes had been crushed and stacked. Bill plucked a whisk broom from a table and presented it for Susanna to grip with her mouth. "Just sweep up in here and you can take your lunch break when you're done." He left, a bounce in his stride.

Dutifully, Susanna began to sweep the concrete floor, herding the bits of tattered cardboard, masking tape, and bubble wrap into larger and larger piles. Stu ignored her, intent on the screen. The store computer regularly got infected by viruses from someone visiting porn sites, and everybody thought it was Stu.

The thought of Cindy and Bobby together made her queasy. She wished she was Cindy, wished Bobby was her boyfriend. It was a painful reminder of what she was missing out on. She tried not to think about it.

Time passed slowly, only interrupted by occasional clicking from the plastic keyboard. Susanna got hungry as her usual lunchtime passed.

Eventually she finished, the debris consolidated into one big pile. She dropped the broom next to it and she crawled back to the break room. From her locker she dragged out a large bag of dry cat food, the only commercial foodstuff her system could digest. She stuck her head in it and ate, crunching loudly. Everyone else had already eaten so the room remained empty.

Moneo said, "The ambassador from Tleilaxu is next."

Susanna sensed something wrong as soon as the short, stocky man with a shaved head entered the chamber, but what? She watched him intently as he approached the Imperial Worm Cart.

"Greetings, my lady," he said, smiling. "Tleilaxu wishes for your continuing health."

A Face Dancer! A shape-changer, one of the various entities Theilaxu created in their axolotl tanks, sent to impersonate the ambassador! He betrayed none of the subtle tell-tale signs, a new development she noted, but the voice had revealed him to her heightened senses.

Susanna sprang from the cart without warning. The assassin only had time to pull the lasgun partway out of his robe before he was crushed by Susanna's massive body. The Face Dancers had limited telepathy to aid their impersonations, but by acting without thinking she had caught him off guard.

Moneo, instantly snapping out of his shock, said, "Is my lady injured?"

"I am unharmed." In truth, she was excited. Something unexpected had happened! Those intermeshing gears of causality bored her. The future they produced was completely predictable, a stifling prison that stretched forever ahead of those who could perceive it. I have the power to smash it! The thought sustained her. Only the unpredictable made her long life interesting enough to bear.

She returned to her cart and pondered the bloody mess on the floor as it floated above the stars.

If only she was a Face Dancer! Susanna wouldn't have to be an earthworm anymore. She could take the shape of anyone, like Cindy or the models on the covers of *Allure* or *Glamour* she had to pass on the magazine racks. And whenever she wanted, she could change again.

A new fantasy took shape, one built around being a Face Dancer, a galactic courtesan who kept her shape-changing and mind-reading abilities secret.

"Hey, Susanna," Bill said, leaning in the door. "Store meeting."

Susanna looked at the wall clock. It was already after six. Her shift was over and it was time to go home.

The staff was gathered around the magazine racks, the largest open space in the store. The crowd was larger than it had been that morning; the evening workers, high school students, had come in, chattering and laughing. Mike, another of the sales associates, dashed off to help a lone customer.

Susanna sat herself in a coil next to Stu and Tracy, a middle-aged woman with jet-black hair and faded punk tattoos.

"Do you know what this is about?" Tracy asked Stu.

"No idea."

"Could I have your attention please?" Bill said in a raised voice. "Could I have quiet?" The high school students hushed in stages as Bill repeated his request.

"I'll make this brief. I've just been on the phone with corporate headquarters. Happyworld has filed for bankruptcy. They've sold all our inventory to another company, so after we close tonight, we're not opening again. Your final paychecks will be mailed to you. Are there any questions?"

Susanna felt as if she was falling. How could she get another job? She couldn't.

People began to talk as the initial shock wore off. The high school students resumed their chatter, but the full-time employees looked glum.

"Welp, it looks like we're out of a job." Stu said to Tracy.

Tracy made a face. "I knew we were doing badly, but I didn't expect this at all."

Susanna wiggled about listening to conversations, but no one spoke to her and eventually she felt so isolated she had to crawl away. No one seemed to notice.

As she passed the front windows, she saw rain streaking brightly past the parking lot lights. In the break room, she dragged the bag of cat food out of her locker and examined it. The thick, glossy paper looked reasonably waterproof, so if she could roll up the top tightly the contents might stay dry and not spoil. She couldn't afford to waste anything now. She clasped the upper edges with her mouth and struggled.

Mike stalked into the break room, his pale redhead's complexion flushed bright pink. He was a Christian and carried a pocket Bible so he could pray for customers. "They're idiots!" he shouted. "I've always said the people running this company were idiots!"

He looked around, glasses catching the fluorescent light, and noticed her. "Susanna! Here, let me help you with that." He knelt down and rolled up the bag for her while she watched gratefully.

"I guess you're really in a jam, being laid off. Do you know what you're going to do?"

Susanna shook her head.

"Well, I'll include you in my prayers. Can you carry that?"

Susanna lifted the bag experimentally. It was heavy, but not too heavy. She nodded.

"Okay! Well, good luck. It's been interesting knowing you."

Susanna crawled across the store and out into the crowds jostling through the mall. "Feliz Navidad" blared from the glittering ceiling. The fountain splashed in the food court. To Susanna, the noise and movement were so distant that the mall seemed as empty as it had been that morning.

On the bus, Susanna found an empty seat and put the bag down on the floor. She looked out the window as the bus followed its route, watching for landmarks in the dark so she wouldn't miss her stop. Thoughts whirled through her mind—*I don't know what to do, my money will run out soon, I'll lose my apartment and be homeless, my life is over*—but she didn't feel anything. That would come later. When they passed the final streetlight, she stretched up and pulled the cord.

From the bus stop, she slithered homeward through the maze of driveways and parking lots that ran through the apartment complex, head bent down to shield the bag from the rain. When a car went by she would wriggle off the pavement and onto the wet lawn to avoid being hit and to dodge the spray from the hissing tires. Sometimes the drivers, seeing something on the road ahead, switched on their high beams, blinding her until they passed.

Inside her building, she inched up two flights of steps and peeked around the corner to make sure the hallway was empty. It was, so she dipped into the nylon bag around her midsection and came out with the key in her mouth. Twisting her head in a practiced movement, she unlocked the door, then pushed it open, forcing it against the clutter on the floor.

She turned on the light. A thick layer of junk covered the entire floor. Most of it was paper: mail, take-out menus she had found wedged in her door, obsolete government forms, old photos. Pages had been torn from the notebooks with her journals and poetry as she crawled around her apartment, too indifferent to pick them up, and the pages gradually crumpled, dirtied, tattered to the point where she couldn't tell what they had been. She always felt a pang of loss when she noticed one. There were half-full trash bags, empty boxes, broken plastic, tangled electrical cords connected to nothing, the female clothing she had bought in anticipation of her new life. Her eyes watered from the dust.

She crawled over to the kitchen and deposited the bag of cat food next to the bag she was using at home. There were empty bags too. She should throw those out, she thought, and take them out to the dumpster later when all the neighbors had gone to sleep. She opened the bag and looked inside. The food was dry. She felt relief, a sense of accomplishment.

The fear hit her like a physical force. The kitchen wavered as her body seemed to dissolve. She felt dizzy, off-balance, as if the room was tilting with nothing anywhere to hang on to.

I need to calm down, she thought. I need to make plans, but the first thing I need to do is to calm down so I can think.

She crawled to the bedroom. Sheets, blankets, pillows lay in a pile on the bare mattress. She burrowed inside them, shutting out the world.

Alarms shrilled throughout the citadel; warning lights flashed. I am under attack, Susanna thought. My rule is threatened. She accelerated her cart down the sloping tunnel, deeper into the defensive fortifications her foresight had provided. When she reached her emergency communications center she would take control and lead a counterattack. Above all I must not give into fear. Fear is the mindkiller!

I don't think you understand what 'attraction' means
Tobi Hill-Meyer

I don't think you understand what 'attraction' means. If you really aren't attracted to trans women, why don't you leave us alone?

You complain that trans women want to 'trick' you into having sex with them, so clearly worried that some girl you're hot for might turn out to be trans. You run through a dozen hypothetical scenarios, dealing out judgment and explaining exactly when and how trans women should disclose. You talk through which sex acts you would be most repulsed by, and how important it is for everyone to protect you from falling into that scenario. Seriously, I don't know about everyone else, but I don't spend this much time talking and thinking about having sex with people I'm not attracted to.

When confronted about your transphobia, your standard response is: "I'm just not attracted to trans women, there's nothing wrong with that." But the whole scenario you're focusing on is *the possibility* that someone you are attracted to turns out to be trans, and you'd go into a rage. If you were not attracted to trans women, wouldn't you have never gone on a date with her to begin with? Because of, you know, not being attracted to her?

How is it that you ended up arguing with a dozen trans women on social media? Somehow you managed to keep up with each of them and know them by name, all so you can better harass them. You leave little remarks on their page about how they are tricking people into sex.

They say the opposite of attraction isn't repulsion but indifference, and you're not acting like someone who is indifferent to trans women. Did you really just say you're not attracted to trans women for the fourth time in this conversation? I'm beginning to wonder that it's not me you're trying to convince, but yourself.

I'm willing to bet that if we could thoroughly explore your computer and your internet history, we'd find some trans porn on there. What? Is that "Research?" Oh, I forgot. It's "evidence." You've got screen caps of at least fifty trans women's OKCupid pages and downloaded copies of their Fetlife photos—all documented with name, age, and location so that you can post them to your own website and "warn" other people so no one is "tricked" into having sex with them. Scouring the internet, you relish every nude pic you can find, each posted to the front page of your site with a triumphant *Look! It's a penis! And she calls herself a woman—HA!*

Usually when someone is not attracted to me, they don't give it a second thought. They move on with the rest of their life and allow me to move on with mine. But you? You track down my personal Internet accounts so you can continue the argument we got into after I left. You go through things I posted on Tumblr three years ago. You look through my online dating profiles from 2010 and run reverse Google image searches to see where else my risqué photos may have been. You check legal name change records in my county to try to find my "real" name. You look up where I work so you can call my boss and tell them that they hired a pervert. You write what amounts to fan fiction about how many cocks you're imagining I suck and send it to the city council and the school board until their lawyers send you a cease and desist letter. (*Seriously, that really happened to me!*)

There's nothing wrong with incidentally not being attracted to me, but that's not what's going on here. I'm not saying you are attracted to me, but in your repulsion you've become obsessed with me and others like me. That obsession is what's dangerous, and it's fueled by some deep-seated fascination that has a lot more to do with your feelings than it has to do with anything I've done.

So, let's be clear—I'm rejecting you, right here and now. *I will never have sex with you.* If you're really not attracted to me, then you won't care. If you feel relief, if you feel anxiety, if you feel insulted, then there's something else going on. And you need to go take care of it by yourself.

Don't involve me.

Failure

Larissa Glasser

"Well my sister just fucking died."

That's how I shared the big news with my family on Facebook, those whom I hadn't blocked by then.

I was sitting alone in my favorite Mexican restaurant just down the block from The Strand. It's pretty much my New York ritual, especially the alone part. I saw an unrecognized missed call on my phone—I usually ignore those. I assumed it was just another telemarketer. However, when I saw where the call was geo-tagged, I had a bad feeling what this was about.

The voice in the message introduced himself as the police chief of L____, Virginia. *Oh shit, great—this is about my sister again.* The cops knew her well. The cop sounded impassive, resigned. His thick, southern drawl would have otherwise given this Yankee trans girl some pause, but I looked around and saw so much of New York City around me, my safest city. With this urban buffer, the cop sounded rather endearing... from a distance. I didn't care for that. My guard is always up, especially with cops.

I knew what the news was going to be.

I had been anticipating my sister's death for weeks. Two of her cis friends living in her town had contacted me on Facebook and implored me to come down where she was living, in Trump-country, and convince her to get help. She was drinking herself to death.

I didn't go, though. I didn't have much time left off of work, even for emergencies. Besides—the last time I'd tried to save her, she yelled at me.

I returned the call. The cop was deferential and polite. He didn't misgender me once. I don't think the pitch of my voice, nor my inflection, were on his mind—I'd just been the only family contact in her phone book. My sister had also estranged herself from most of my family, but for different reasons than I.

She was my oldest sibling. She changed my diapers. She was into rock-and-roll and Shakespeare. She was my earliest source of blonde envy (*I'm brunette*).

The cops found her unresponsive in her bed. Her house was full of trash, feces, and empty bottles of vodka and wine. They wanted me to come down to claim her body. I explained that I wasn't able to at the moment, but that I would take whatever information they had. They gave me the number to their town morgue and asked me to give that information to my brother. He lives in Puerto Rico, even further away from Virginia than me.

After I hung up, I looked around at Manhattan again. I realized that I was visiting the same city that my nephew (*my sister's only son*) had fatally overdosed five years before. Compounded with the death of her husband, and then of her son, these things had tapped my sister's will to live.

I hadn't spoken with my nephew since right after I transitioned. He never said much to me, and I had been floating away from most of my family for the sake of my autonomy and sanity. Still, when I got the news about his overdose, I felt more traces of myself being ripped away.

And now this.

I contacted my brother and gave him the details about the morgue. He'd been trying to save her as well, but he struggles with health and mobility issues of his own. I told him what was up with me (not much, except that I didn't want to return to Boston, I never do), and asked if there was going to be a wake for her. I wanted to at least know. He didn't answer at the time, and he never did tell me. I still wonder to this day if they held one and just didn't invite me. Maybe I'm just being paranoid about that.

My mom never wanted to talk about my sister. During the months leading up to my sister's death, they fought a lot and both used me as a quasi-ambassador. My sister was convinced that she'd never been told who her real father was. I empathized with her because my own birth had been a matter of scandal (*I'm a cheat baby—my mom fucked my dad when she was still married to the Nantucket Chief of Police—what is it with me and cops LOL*). But I also knew my sister was belligerent and hot-headed when she drank. I tried so hard to solve their differences, but I couldn't. And eventually, something terrible sank in as to why I was powerless to do so.

See, for years, my mom and my sister had used my being trans as ammunition against each other. When having a disagreement over something, they would both weaponize my transition as a means to hurt the other, usually with accusations of failure back and forth. *As if I had no agency in the matter.*

This always happened outside my presence, of course, but I caught wind of it from the rest of my family. My sister knew how to hurt my mom, so she would use me as cudgel. This didn't really bother me so much until after my sister died, though, when I had the benefit of hindsight. And still, there was so much I had wanted to try and help her with. But my mom hasn't been talking to me lately and I blame myself for not being able to help save my sister.

I don't regret transitioning, but the fact that my family uses it to make me feel guilty—to blame me for the problems they experience but don't take responsibility for—bums me the fuck out. If you ask me, my transition ruled in that it gave me some distance from my family (*which is a **huge** perk*). But I'd never wanted to completely shake *all of them* loose. My sister and brother had remained close with me through most of it.

The last time I spoke with my sister on the phone, her house was reported to me as being choked with garbage from floor to ceiling. Her own phone and utilities had been shut off. Her ex-boyfriend called me from her front porch as we tried to strategize how to get through to her. He went inside and handed his phone to her. I admit, I'd tried to give her some tough love on that phone call. I asked her why she wouldn't let us get her into assisted living, where at least the staff had the option of taking care of her needs.

Then the yelling started. I didn't know how much she had been drinking, but the loudness and anger in her voice spoke volumes. I pleaded with my sister to call me the next day when she felt more calm.

That was the last time I ever talked to her.

By the time my lunch came to me in that Manhattan restaurant,

I glared at the nice tall glass of Merlot I had ordered. It might have been my second. Maybe third.

I thought of my dead dad, my dead nephew, my dead sister. I felt dead to the world.

I contemplated the spiral sucking at my feet. It was inviting me to join the ranks of the dead in a warm place where we'd not have to feel so many terrible things. I don't even know why I should give such a fuck about my sister. She was so into her own shit that, by the end, her old love and begrudging acceptance for me wasn't enough to let me help her. Maybe that's what I have to look forward as I keep getting older. Will I become her? Am I becoming her now? Will I be so fed up with everything and numb to everyone around who has ever "loved" me, including the family who judged me for being a "monster," that I will fade away like her, my dad, and my nephew?

Ultimately, I know that I am not to blame for my sister's death. Still, I can't completely shake the lie that this was, and is, my fault. No matter what my brain tells me, or what my collective trauma is, I did not deserve the bad things that happened to me, and neither did she. She deserves to be alive, and so do I. But the demons and abuse we both faced are now hardwired thoughts within our nervous systems. Maybe that's why I care about her so much. We both turned into addicts because we just wanted to *not feel* that way anymore. Does anyone?

I'm honestly tempted to just say "fuckit" about the whole thing, but that's what my sister did—she said *fuckit*. And I'm still here.

So even if I still think I failed my sister, that doesn't mean I have to keep failing myself.

Hormones
Serafima Mintz

The feeling of waking up next to Gordon on the crinkly, plastic-wrapped twin-sized mattress of his motel bedroom, my thigh pressed into the chasm of his crotch, watching his roaring exhales bristle through the hairs of his thin moustache as he moaned softly in his sleep, was not magic. There wasn't a feeling of excitement or budding infatuation, or a longing for the moment to last, though I'm apt to have those feelings when the moment and person are right. But Gordon did seem peaceful laying there, gratified by our night of indulgence, where he was indulged, lavishly, again and again, by me. And I was happy to give him that, proud of my penchant to gratify and skill in pleasing. I was glad to see the calm was still upon him.

I wake up at seven o'clock every morning nearly on the dot without an alarm, which is helpful for work—I work at a preschool—but annoying on the weekends, because I never sleep enough, though really who does? I've been an early riser since long before I started working. I looked at the clock and it was seven, on the dot, and I didn't want to disturb Gordon, but I also needed relief from his grip and his wheezing. There was an acrid smell in the air that overpowered the rot from Gordon's fridge, which overwhelmed me when combined with Gordon's breath. I disentangled myself from his arms, legs, and semi-erection. I pulled on my dress and grabbed his ashtray, walked it out the door to the dumpster outside, past a shuffleboard court and three or four barren coconut trees. There were mattresses piled up next to the dumpster—I counted six while I emptied the ashtray—and there were four people, all above sixty, tough-looking and sunburnt, sitting on lawn chairs scattered in a cluster on the blue concrete. They were all smoking. Not talking, just smoking, so I sat down—not among them, but on the other side of the courtyard—and started smoking, too. The ashtray was on my lap, and I kept flicking the cigarette into it, after every inhale; flick, flick, drag; flick, flick, drag. Gordon poked his head out of his door when I was almost finished, wearing a towel, motioning for me to come inside. "I have to go," he said. "Can you get in here?"

I obliged. I walked inside, grabbed my purse, placed Gordon's ashtray back down on my nightstand. "Gren," he said. "Is it Gren?" I nodded. "That was great," he said. "I needed that."

"I needed that, too," I said, because I meant it.

"I'd like to do that again sometime, if you would like to."

"I would like to," I said, because I did.

And then he handed me eighty dollars, and I asked, "Why?" Because we had never talked about him paying me.

He looked nervous. "Well, just in case in you need it."

To which I answered, "Thank you, I do."

We had met innocently the night before, at a bar that I had went to with my sister, who only stayed for half an hour, not being a drinker, but easily bored. I stayed beyond that, because it was Friday night, and after half an hour I was already drunk. Gordon sat next to me almost as soon as my sister left and started chatting me up. I liked it. A lot, at first. He had this pleasant and free way about him, as if no big troubles in his life had yet taught him to be bitter or mute, and he had a cute moustache, which was nice because I like moustaches. He had a smile that said, "I'm non-threatening," and a sweater that said, "I have money," and he treated me with an overt kindness that I took as genuine at the time. He looked like he was maybe twenty-three, though I later found out he was twenty-nine, and he acted like he was forty, which I found charming for some reason. He bought me a drink, which was a big deal to me, because I was only twenty and had to use an embarrassing fake ID to buy one myself, and he told me all about his life, totally unprovoked by me. I took this for confidence at the time, though it might have been more his self-obsession.

He had a French Canadian accent with a sort of swagger to it, and he told me he had just moved here from Montreal. He had a degree in entrepreneurial arts and planned to use it to follow what he said was his lifelong dream—to run his father's motel, the Aloha Motel, in Hollywood, Florida. It didn't have a pool, but it was going to have a pool. He had big plans, he said. The first step was getting rid of the bed bugs. I nodded, and he went on and on and on. He said that Hollywood was a hub for Quebecers, who would stay at motels for months at a time in the winter. They wanted the full South Florida experience, with a Quebecois twist.

Gordon asked me about the Florida experience. He asked, "Where would you take somebody who knows nothing, like me?" and he smiled in this sly and innocent way. It made me honestly consider where I would take him. There was the beach off of Las Olas where all the palm trees twist in the wind, and, further south, the canoe trails in West Lake Park. I thought about the science museum. Would a Quebecois tourist be interested in the science museum? He said, *yes, of course. We should go tomorrow.* And we both laughed, and I thought, *was that funny?*

I didn't put up any resistance when Gordon asked me to go back to his place, to his room, which he assured me was bed-bug free. And though I was drunk, I enjoyed the sex thoroughly. Gordon did not seem to care much about me personally, and he didn't seem interested in who I was as a human being. He didn't ask me where I work, or what I like to do on my free time. But he appreciated my body in a way it seemed that no one did, like he needed it, and had been missing it all his life. He embraced me hungrily, demanding that I use him as I pleased, and he held my hand around the back of his neck while I kissed him. He worshipped me, begging for me to explode wherever I wanted, as I rubbed all of myself over all of him. And I did explode, at the same time that he did, and he ate it, and then we ate Chinese delivery. It was great, which was why, though perhaps quite thrilled with the experience, I was perturbed about what happened the next morning.

I asked my sister about it later, when I got back to our house from Gordon's. My sister is also an early riser, and when I got home, she was already up and working, her computer out and in front of her on the table, her earphones with the microphone on and buzzing. She works for AT&T, sending people on frustrating telephone loops in hopes that they will give up and stop complaining. Or, that's what the company hopes. Mischa likes to help as much as she can.

Like me, my sister is transgender, but two years younger. She works, and couldn't not work, but she works at home, not because that's what she wants for herself, but because she is afraid of the dangers, real and perceived, that lurk in the alternatives. She's at a stage where she both loves and fears her own trans-ness. She is an expert on astrology and gossip, invaluable to consult with on matters of the heart.

When she saw me walk in, Mischa wrapped up her conversation with the customer she was working with—"You're going to have to talk with Billing about that," I think I heard her say—and she took off her headset. I asked her if she was allowed to do that, and she said no, but it doesn't really matter, because she just puts everyone on hold anyway. She asked me what's up. "You weren't home last night."

"Yeah," I said. "I know." I talk to my sister honestly and forthrightly, always. I trust her to listen when I tell her what's on my mind. I said, "Mischa, I had sex with a man last night, and in the morning he gave me eighty dollars."

"Okay," Mischa said, looking concerned.

"I didn't expect it, though. I was confused. I didn't mention wanting money."

"Oh, dear," Mischa said. "That does sound confusing."

Has that ever happened to you? Are men just like that? I wanted to ask those questions to my sister, who shares so much with me in outlook and experience. I couldn't ask, though; a quiet shame restrained me. I whimpered.

Mischa got up from her chair and sat next to me on the couch, patting my back in a circular, motherly motion. And, as if from a mother, I recoiled, fearing what feelings could be triggered by sharing the details of dangerous or unpleasant situations. "This sounds intense, Gren," Mischa said. "Do you want me to call in sick from work? We can talk for a while. I'll make you eggs."

"Oh Mischa," I said, "I don't know." I looked away, trying to hide an emotion I took for embarrassment, while Mischa kept rubbing my back. "Do you think this is really that weird?" I asked. "Is it even that out of the ordinary? Because in the back of my mind I was half-expecting it, him believing that my body was for sale. I feel that so often in the way that people talk to me, and the way they look at me. Like there's this secret loathing or lust behind every just-too-sustained passing glance. It's because I'm trans, I guess. Or, because I look trans. And don't you feel that, too, sometimes?" I asked my sister. "Isn't it awful?"

"Yes," Mischa said. "I do. It is." She patted my shoulder. "This is very distressing, Gren. Are you doing okay?"

"Yes, I am, and it's no big deal. Please go back to work, Mischa. Please."

And she did. "I'm sorry for the wait, sir. Please calm down." I heard the voice on the other line: "Don't tell *me* to calm down, sir. I've been on hold for forty-five minutes."

My poor sister. Fuck, I love her so much.

All I could think about was Gordon, alternating lustful and spiteful thoughts that were hard to control, so I thought about my sister. I let myself focus on her voice while she talked with her customers, felt her frustration. I closed my eyes and imagined faraway people with faulty wi-fi. I allowed my thoughts to flow naturally to the epicenter of my anxiety—my needs, the needs of my sister, and the specter of meeting all of those needs. I focused on the biggest unmet need, which was hormones. Mischa and I both needed hormones, desperately.

I used the data from my cell phone to look up doctors, but couldn't find any that I hadn't called before. No endocrinologists, gynecologists, or primary care physicians. None with any specialty in "transgender issues." None who will see new patients, let alone patients with no insurance. Perhaps I should have come out when I had insurance, before I turned eighteen. Perhaps I should have been born in San Francisco. I looked up getting estrogen from Mexico online. I found nothing. Also nothing in Canada. I had heard stories of that working, people getting them online. Perhaps those people understand how to use BitCoins.

I couldn't find any immediate means toward getting hormones, and it was frustrating, so I just lay there on the couch next to Mischa and listened to her sweet voice. "I understand that your Internet's out, sir, but I'm afraid I've done all I can do from here. If you'd like, we can send a technician to your residence to check on your connection. That will come at a fee of fifty dollars." I fell asleep and didn't wake up until it was dark out. Mischa made us eggs and we played Zelda on her laptop. I thought about bringing up Gordon again and what happened with him. Should I have retuned the eighty dollars? Should I have left in a puff, offended? Rhetorical questions I decided against asking. I just sat with it, letting the feelings simmer throughout the week.

Thoughts about Gordon would pop up amid the most random of situations—at work when I was changing diapers, bored but nurturing, slightly disgusted; or when I was supervising nap time; or when I was driving past the restaurant that serves poutine. I was thinking about him more than I intended. My romantic encounters, to tell the truth, have been few and far between. It's very rare—I once thought impossible—for a man to charm me and make me feel beautiful. Gordon did, I had to admit, at least for one night. And he paid me. But did that ruin it?

I didn't know, but I was relieved when he called me the next Friday. I didn't remember giving him my number, but I must have. He sounded happy, but also like he was trying to speak as quietly as possible.

"So, do you want to meet up?" It felt nice to hear his Canadian accent.

"Yes," I said. "Sure, why not? When and where?"

And he said, "Just come here in an hour."

So I said, "Okay."

When I got to his motel room, he had a meat-lovers pizza out and open with four of the slices gone, and his TV was on—something about alien conspiracies. We watched it for twenty minutes or so while I ate pizza and talked at the TV, just to make conversation, because he wasn't talking much. He seemed nervous, much more so than the previous week. He was chain smoking, and he kept running his fingers through his hair, which was full, and pulling out chunks of dandruff or maybe psoriasis and wiping them off on his plastic mattress cover. I kissed him first and took off my shirt, and then he loosened up and took off his. He started touching me, pushing me into the bed with his palms while I wriggled underneath him. And then I pushed back on him, and got him pinned, and felt at his parts with my foot. It felt nice. The sex was good a second time. It was far from love and barely intimate, but the desire was strong. I felt wanted. He wanted me. I wanted him. Gordon felt grateful for my presence and that was enough. I fell asleep in his bed.

And in the morning, when I woke up at seven, he was already up, this time dressed, with eighty dollars in one hand and his cell phone in the other, talking to someone about a sod delivery or something. I got dressed slowly, and he hung up by the time I was done.

"Hey, Gren, listen, thanks, hon. That was great," he said. I felt special, in a way, when he called me "hon." "Maybe meet again next week?"

I said, "For sure."

He held out four twenties, and I hesitated, internally only. Outwardly, nearly automatically, I reached out and grabbed the cash.

"Thanks, Gordon. I appreciate this."

He didn't smile, but he did wave as I walked past him and out into the light of the motel plaza.

I drove home, slept until noon, and felt okay, a little energized. I expended the energy on the Internet doing nothing. I put the money Gordon had given me in an envelope in my closet. I thought, this is good, this thing with Gordon. I'm making money. *Ha!* I thought. *The joy of being wanted.*

The week after having seen Gordon, one of the kids at the preschool bit me. He was having a meltdown, and meltdowns are common, but this was the big one of the week. I was trying to change him and he bit my calf out of spite at his discomfort. There had been a long line of toddlers to change, and he was the last. He pulled me down with the full force of his jaw toward the ground, jumping head-first into the carpet. He ripped off a chunk, and I got to go home early. We were all relieved that no one was seriously hurt. I drove straight to the beach from work and washed my wound off in the ocean, and I called Gordon, just to see what he was up to. He answered immediately to say, "I'll call you back," then he hung up and didn't call me until Saturday evening, when I was busy, out getting groceries with Mischa. We were getting plantains, four for a dollar, and deciding whether to get yellow or green. I said green, because I like the green ones better, and if we don't use them soon, they'll just turn yellow.

"And then they'll turn black," my sister said. "Sweet, like me."

My phone rang.

"Hey," I said. "What's up? I'm in the store."

"Oh, just saying hello." It was Gordon. "I can call back if this isn't a good time."

"Oh, no," I said, "It's fine," I felt a kind of confidence over the phone, able to speak to Gordon calmly despite my sister's wild gesturing, who is that? "Do you want to meet tonight?"

"Oh, yes, please," he said. "Yes, I would." He stumbled over his words; again that nervousness. I think some people might have been turned off by his uncomfortable desperation, because it *was* uncomfortable, but I wasn't turned off. I found it charming.

"Oh, great," he said, "I'll get us sushi." And I wanted to tell him I don't like fish, but he had hung up.

"Well who was that?" asked my sister.

"That was that guy. The one from two weeks ago."

"Oh, *that* guy?" she said, digging to the bottom of the plantain pyramid. "You're seeing him?"

"Yeah."

"Oh, okay."

And I thought my sister was going to press me, ask me tons of questions, like, why? and um, what? But she didn't. Because my sister is a gentle, empathic creature, and she can tell when I'm feeling secretive. She just put two green plantains and two almost rotten brown plantains in the shopping cart and started arguing with me about which cheese to get.

My sister. Fuck, I love her.

I didn't hurry Mischa in the grocery store. She took her usual fifty to seventy minutes deciding on the most delicious and economical cereals, the right size and flavor of ice cream, the proper number of frozen hot dogs. Also which kind of buns. She kept finding cracks in eggs, which she says is a relief, because could you imagine the alternative, finding out at home? We had to put things back that we couldn't afford on our EBT card. Overall, a very usual shopping trip. After we checked out, got home, unpacked our groceries; I showered, put on make-up, usual things. I got to Gordon's house near midnight and he was sitting on the floor watching Seinfeld. His eyes looked misty, like he had been crying, and I asked him what's wrong.

"Nothing's wrong," Gordon said, kind of sighing. He handed me a half-eaten platter of sushi and he smiled in a fake way, like, "you should feel guilty," and I did. I had kept him waiting for a very long time. I accepted the sushi graciously, ate a few bites, and then I started taking off my shirt. I kissed Gordon's neck and he seemed to relax.

But only a little. Up until that point Gordon had wilted at my touch, seemed to beg for it with his eyes. Just wiggling a little in front of him would make him submit. But that night he seemed to resist. When I put my arm to his ribs, he forced the weight of his whole torso into it, and he grabbed my hand as if to hold it there, but then he let go, like he had just remembered something troubling. I kept kissing him, wanting to see him lose himself. To forget whatever it was, remember only the bliss of my body. He did think it was blissful, I thought. He had felt that only one week before. But now he couldn't sustain that feeling. It made me feel sheepish, annoyed, and self-conscious. He didn't even reach over to turn off the TV. He didn't make any requests, things that he wanted me to do. I licked all of his favorite lickable parts, and he barely reacted. He didn't cum.

He just said, "Oh, yeah, not in the mood I guess. Thanks for coming, though. Really appreciate it." He was disinterested, and I didn't understand it. If he had called me, wasn't it because he wanted to see me? He handed me forty dollars, which I didn't question, though which did, in fact, offend me; I left and the sun just beginning to set as I got home.

I wanted to talk to Mischa, just to vent. Because fuck, this guy. First he wants me, then he doesn't. But Mischa was asleep.

That's not out of the ordinary for her, to be fast asleep around seven p.m. With her job, she has the luxury of setting her own schedule, the logic of which eludes me. She prefers long shifts, twelve hours if possible, three times a week, plus a four-hour shift some other day.

Sometimes, on the last day, she'll do sixteen. I supposed she had just stopped working recently, after having worked all of the night before.

I share a bed with Mischa, but I didn't want to wake her. I have a small AM/FM radio that I keep in my purse because the one in my car is broken, and I took that out and listened with my headphones to pass the time, unable to rest. I listened to the public radio newscast and tried to focus on all of that misery, that grief, of bombed-out hospitals in Aleppo, a pipeline explosion, poisoned water. I couldn't, my petty problems screaming too loudly. Because what went wrong? Was it because I was late? Was it because it took so long for me to call?

Mischa woke up around two in the morning and nearly immediately started crying.

"Oh, honey," I said. "What's wrong?"

Mischa was making a type of face that she never likes other people to see, because despite being gentle, she would like to be unwaveringly strong. She is strong, but not as much as she would like to be. She doesn't complain much, no matter how awful the situation. But her face was contorted in a way that looked like she was in pain, like there was a spike in her foot or her gut was bleeding. "Gren," she said, "I'm just so exhausted." She huffed.

I asked her what had happened, if there was a customer who was rude to her, or something else. She insisted it was nothing specific, talking to her thumbs, which were rubbing each other. She had the look of a frightened child, or a frightened parent. "I just want a different life, Gren. I'm not happy."

It was like daggers in my heart, but I understood. Mischa barely left the house, isolating herself off even sometimes from me, and she didn't make efforts to make new friends, or to have a love life. She saw both of those things as endlessly complicated, which I guess in a way was reasonable, but it was also because she felt so insecure in herself. Not in who she was as a person, but in the way she looked. How she looked didn't match the way she felt, and she was reminded of that multiple times a day. She had the type of persistent dysphoria that incapacitates nearly totally. But she usually smiles through it. That day she wasn't.

"I was watching this video," Mischa said. "This fourteen-year-old.

Look."

She turned on a YouTube video of a young trans girl who was documenting her transition, and in this video she was describing the pain of her growing breasts. "My nipples," she said. "They just hurt so bad." What was remarkable was the way the girl in the video was laughing through it. Like, ow, my nipples hurt. That means I'm going to have boobs. Hooray! It was a feeling that I wished I could relate to, and I could see where Mischa was going by showing me this video, with this young girl grabbing her budding breasts so joyously.

"I want that, too." Mischa was holding my arm, sitting very close. "I want that nipple pain. I want that smile."

"I know," I told her. "I want that, too." And I wanted to say to my sister, *Hey, Mischa, don't worry, it'll happen.* And I wanted to give her details, like when and where, and have it be real. But I couldn't do that, so I went to the kitchen and made her eggs, and we both ate and then went to sleep. I spent the rest of the week feverishly planning how to get hormones for my sister and myself.

I didn't want to call any doctors. I had already tried that and it had led nowhere. And I worried. Even if we were to find a doctor who would help us, and even if they did write us the prescriptions we needed, how would we pay for those prescriptions and all of the follow-up visits? How would we pay for the blood work every three months? Mischa and I both work. I work about thirty hours a week; Mischa works forty hours a week, every week, for $8.15 an hour. I make nine dollars an hour. Together that's $2,384 dollars per month, which after taxes comes out to about $1,800. Our rent is one thousand dollars per month after our aid from Section 8, for a one-bedroom house with a hot pot instead of a stovetop or oven in the kitchen. We spend about one hundred dollars a week on food, which leaves four hundred dollars for other things—utilities, Internet, gas, thrifted clothing, candles from the dollar store, food for Mischa's goldfish. There is nothing left over, ever, as a rule. We try to prevent it, both Mischa and I, but we're always broke.

I did, however, have two hundred dollars—the money that Gordon gave me—that I never touched. It was just sitting there, in an envelope in my closet. I thought, *there can't be any way a doctor would charge more than a hundred dollars for a visit.* I thought, *if I can pay, then surely they would see Mischa and me.* Unsustainable or not, I figured it would be worth it to take the risk, to get us on hormones as soon as I could, worry about follow-up visits and any future expenses as they come.

But still, when I made calls on my Tuesday, Wednesday, and Thursday lunch breaks, I found no doctors who would see us. Dr. Sloan told me to call Dr. Nason, and Dr. Nason asked if I'd called Dr. Sloan. Dr. Domini said that he would like to help, but his hands were tied. Can't see patients without insurance. I understood. Dr. Saunders was, as usual, out of the office, so I left a message that was never returned.

Mischa's funk got worse. She slept a lot, most of the time she wasn't working. She watched TV alone, on her computer, instead of with me. It was hurting me, seeing my sister so sad, so I was grateful that Friday night when Gordon called me wanting me to come over.

It surprised me, yes, that Gordon had called me, being how uninterested he was the last time, but everything about Gordon had been unpredictable. I had stopped trying to interpret his actions. I just felt good, hopeful because Gordon sounded happy, and I wanted the sex, and the power that it made me feel the first two times. I wanted to wash away the confusing feelings of the previous week. When I put on makeup, it took me twenty minutes, so I called when I was done. "I just spent twenty minutes putting on makeup. I'm leaving now, though." When I got there, he was happy to see me. He was so, so horny.

He had a visible erection from the moment I walked in, and he didn't have food out, and the TV was off. He led me to his bed and he started undressing me right away. It was unrestrained passion, and exactly what I wanted. He kissed me, licked me, held me, asked me to hold him while he came, and I did so happily, helping him clean up when he was finished.

And then his excitement started waning, and he was the Gordon from the previous week, acting standoffish and quiet, pulling away from my kisses. I asked if he wanted me to leave and he didn't say anything. So I said, "Okay, I'm gonna leave," and I did.

Gordon said, "Okay, that's fine," and he handed me eighty dollars. And I took it, added it to the two hundred I had saved, and I resolved not to think about Gordon or his fickle mood until whenever he called me again, because I knew he would, remembering how much he wanted me. I was of value. Eighty dollars worth. I didn't think about what it was that was making him so uncomfortable. Maybe something unrelated, perhaps.

I was still worried about my sister, her mood. The following Monday I called Dr. Saunders, who still did not answer, and I felt dejected, because Dr. Saunders seemed like the last hope. He was not in on Tuesday, either, or on Wednesday. They must be a real doctor's office, I figured, or why would they have a voicemail? I didn't know what to do.

I felt lost and fucking stressed out, and it was out of that feeling that I called Gordon on Wednesday night. Because if he's not going to love me, or really like me, or whatever, he at least, I figured, should help me.

To be clear, I didn't think that Gordon cared about me. His actions led me to believe that, deep down, he didn't. But he owned and managed a motel. He had resources. He was one of the only people I knew with any resources.

He was in a good mood when he picked up the phone. There was hockey on in the background. He seemed undisturbed when I didn't immediately ask to come see him.

"Hey, Gordon," I said. "How are you doing? I hope everything's well. I wanted to talk to you, Gordon. I'm feeling distraught. I just wanted to talk. Is it okay if we just talk for a second, Gordon? Is that okay?" I was nervous.

But he just said, "Sure, what's up?" Unemotional. Confident.

"I need hormones, Gordon," I said. "I can't get them anywhere."

There was a pause. "Oh, hormones," Gordon said. "You can't get them?"

"No," I said. "I can't. I've never been able. Neither me or my sister."

"Oh," Gordon said. "Never? You've never been on hormones?"

"Never."

Gordon said, "Oh." I could almost feel his mood starting to shift over the telephone, but maybe that was just my projection because his voice didn't change. It stayed relatively monotone. He said, "Okay, I think I can help." He told me that he has a way of getting prescription drugs from Canada, from his father's doctor, who he said would write prescriptions for anything, for anyone. *It was how he got his pain pills*, he said, *for when his prescription ran out after his knee surgery.* "I don't know how I would handle the pain," he said, "without dilaudid. Besides, this hook-up is a great way to make extra cash." He told me he would call his dad, who would call his doctor, and then he would call me back within a week, and I couldn't have been more thrilled at his eagerness to help. I asked for a two years' supply of injectable estradiol and a two years' supply of spironolactone. I figured I'd ask for as much as I could, take whatever I could get. I didn't believe that I would get all of that, or really any. Gordon seemed taken aback—he actually whistled over the phone—but he said okay. "I'll see what I can do."

I was skeptical, but Gordon called me back the next day to tell me everything was a go. "Okay, I ordered them," he said. "Everything should be here next week." And I felt elated, then astonished, then concerned. "It's going to cost four thousand dollars, U.S."

"Holy shit," I said. "Thank you so much." Holy shit, I thought, because how would I ever find four thousand dollars? But when I told Mischa that night she seemed unconcerned.

"Four thousand dollars?" she said. "No problem."

I asked if she had any savings.

"No," she told me, "but that doesn't matter. I know how we can do this." She took out her computer and showed me her open tabs. There were pages and pages of trans women soliciting money for their various medical needs, on sites like Kickstarter, IndieGoGo, GoFundMe. Sallie from Spokane was offering hand-carved wooden plaques with the phrase "Love Wins" to anyone who donated fifty dollars toward her vaginoplasty. Becky from Boca Raton was giving out beaded necklaces in exchange for the means toward laser hair removal.

"We just have to make a video," she said. "We can use my cell phone. I can draw pictures for anyone who donates money." My sister draws excellent pictures of Garfield the Cat with his tongue out riding a skateboard, but even if she wrote "Trans Liberation" on the bottom in bright, cute, multicolored bubble letters, I wasn't sure that would make people want to help us. Still I agreed; Mischa was right, it was our best option. We had to reach out to strangers. I hated it.

I wasn't in the video very much, just for a second to say, "My name is Gren and I really need hormones," but the video was long, almost four minutes, mostly of Mischa zooming in and out on her chest—she was wearing a bra—while "Dude Looks Like a Lady" by Aerosmith played in the background. It was great. My sister, she's a genius.

In the first day, we got sixty-five dollars—fifteen dollars from our friend Satya and fifty dollars from anonymous. *That was nice of Satya, I thought, who I know has not much hirself to give.* That was nice of anonymous, whoever they are. I knew it wasn't enough to get us what we needed, but I didn't say anything because Mischa wasn't losing hope and I didn't want to make her.

But I was nervous when Gordon called me on Friday night and I didn't have the money. The hormones hadn't arrived yet, though; he just wanted to see me. Yes, I told him, I'd like to see you very much. And I did. I wanted to see him. He was helping me out. I wanted to kiss him. But I was nervous, so I bought a bottle of cognac on the way over. I don't drink much, but I knew one store that would sell me liquor. Cognac seemed fancy, and it was French. I hoped Gordon would like it.

He did like it. When I put the cognac down on the table next to his bed when I arrived, he made a big deal of me bringing a gift. "Oh, how lovely," he said. "From France! This is the good stuff." He offered to pour me a shot, and he poured one for both of us, which we both drank. "This is good," he said. "Really good."

He started telling me about his day, his month, and all of his problems. He talked about tenants that wouldn't pay, a construction crew that never showed, and the problem of bed bugs, which was now more pressing than ever. He laughed when he told me about a woman who was staying in one of the suites, whose cat got stuck in her cat door. "This cat was so fat," he said. "He was just shaking his fat arms and legs. We had to use Crisco to get him out, and he wailed like crazy."

The image horrified me, but I was glad that, at the moment, Gordon and I were talking, like we had when we first met—like we were equals and relatable human beings. Or not like that exactly, but at least like I was someone to impress.

I only drank one more shot, but Gordon finished off the rest of the bottle, and it was exciting when he picked me up and threw me on his bed. We had great sex and he passed out immediately after, with my arms wrapped around his body, where they stayed until morning, when he woke up, at six, saying he had to go.

"Sorry to do this, hon," he said, not looking at all sorry. "I got a meeting, with the cleaning people. I gotta go." He already had his eighty dollars out and he was holding them toward my face. The money tickled my nose, and I laughed. Without thinking about anything, I started talking.

"Oh, I don't need that, Gordon. I'm here because I want to see you. I'm not here for the money, really. I'm just here for us."

I closed my eyes, still drowsy, but Gordon shook me and said, "Get up." Not like angry, he just said it. "Get up." He put his money away and went into the bathroom, and I sat on his bed wondering why I said what I said, or if I meant it, or how Gordon took it. He stayed in the bathroom for a while. I got dressed, picked up the empty bottle of Cognac and threw it into the garbage. I waited for Gordon until he got out, and he said, "What the fuck do you mean, 'us?'"

I felt regret at what I had said, then seeing the anger in Gordon's eyes. "There is no 'us,'" he said. "I'm not your boyfriend. I'm not a faggot!" And then he pushed me out the door, both elbows stretched out in front of him, and he threw his eighty dollars in a wad onto the motel courtyard. "You're not even on hormones," he yelled through the door. "You fucking guy!"

I drove home in a fury, didn't bother turning on my handheld radio, just muttered to myself, "Gordon, that motherfucker. That mother*fucker*!" When I got to my driveway I saw that he had sent me a text that just said, "sorry. i was way rude." *Fucking right you were. Sorry my ass.* I slammed the front door behind me when I got home, which knocked Mischa's drawings off the table, which made me feel bad and disrupted my anger. Because Mischa was just like, "Hey, Gren. I made eggs."

I said, "Mischa, thank you, I'm sorry," and I walked into the bedroom and closed the door behind me. I texted back, "will u still get me hormones." He replied, "ya." Fucking great.

I walked back into the living room. I said, "Mischa, I love you. I love your ideas. I love your drawings. But please take your video off of the Internet. I have a different idea."

She asked, "What?"

And I said, "Fuck it, I'm going to steal 'em."

And she looked at me. "From that guy?" she said. "That sounds good. Yeah, okay."

So I called our friend Satya, who told me to come over that evening.

Satya is my one true ride or die outside of my sister, a friend since high school and fellow gender outcast—a truly lovely person who is really, truly neither man nor woman, but sharp-witted, caring, and fiercely reserved. To the ones ze loves, Satya will give the world. To the rest of everybody, ze sells. Satya sells guns. I don't know for how long ze has, but for a while. That's why I called hir. Satya told me ze had a gun that ze would lend me.

And when I got to Satya's house, the gun was already out, in pieces on Satya's mattress, the only piece of furniture in Satya's room, and Satya was leaning over its parts, eyes transfixed, rubbing each one with a microfiber cloth. There was a look of concentration in Satya's eyes that one might expect on a surgeon or jeweler, and there was a purposefulness to hir actions that made me feel like I was intruding. I felt like maybe I should have knocked, and I said so.

"Oh, no," Satya said, looking up with hir warm, toothy smile. "If I had wanted you to knock, I would have locked the door." And ze hugged me. Because we always hug. And if the door to Satya's apartment is unlocked, ze has told me before, it is okay to enter without knocking. Please do. Satya's hug had the soft clenching power of a cotton sweater. It helped me. Satya noticed my nervousness and began showing me the gun like it was one of Satya's friends I hadn't met, but would be glad to. Ze picked up the parts and started clunking them together. Spring into cylinder, grip into barrel, magazine. Clunk.

"This is an Uzi," Satya said, seeming proud. "It is a very effective weapon." It looked like a pistol, but like a machine gun. Both at once. I was stunned. Satya held it out to me on two palms, then ze placed it back on hir bed and said, "Please, sit down." I did immediately, both out of trust in Satya and respect, or maybe fear, of the Uzi that ze was holding. Satya looked calm.

"This has three settings." Ze pointed to a switch above the grip. "'A,' 'R,' 'S.'" It was switched to "S." "'S' is the safety," Satya said. "When it's on 'S,' it won't shoot." Ze didn't flip the switch, but moved hir finger as if ze was going to, making sure I was watching, guiding with hir eyes. "'R.' The 'R' stands for reflex, or semi-automatic. When it's on 'R' it will shoot one time, whenever you pull the trigger." I nodded, imagining Satya out at the shooting range to which ze had taken me once, wearing goggles and earplugs, pressing the Uzi into hir muscular, 300-pound body, shooting ten bullets, one by one, through the direct center of a target, smiling.

"Got it, 'R,'" I said, much slower than I speak usually, imagining myself in the same shooting range, shooting once and flailing back into the wall behind me.

"Cool." Satya made like ze was flipping the switch to "A." "This is what's special about the Uzi," Satya said. "This 'A' is what makes the gun illegal in most states, but not in Florida. Other guns this size don't have this." Satya tried to prove the point. Ze took out a duffel bag from underneath hir bed and ze unzipped it. This was a bag that ze had shown me before, when I had asked, curious about what ze had done with hir day, when on that day ze had happened to sell a gun, or many guns. The bag was filled with a wide variety of guns.

"You see these?" Satya said. "These are garbage, all of them. I mean, they're not garbage. But they're garbage against an Uzi."

I said okay.

Ze said okay also and zipped up the bag. "When it's on 'A,'" ze said, "it shoots 500 rounds per minute." And right away I started doing the math. That would be eight rounds per second, or twenty-four rounds in three seconds, which means that in three seconds I could accidentally shoot somebody twenty-four times, then end up in prison for twenty-five years to life, which would mean a minimum of 9,130 days.

I said, "Okay," to the bed, to the Uzi, and then, "Do I really need that?" to Satya.

Satya considered for a while, then said, "Well, tell me about this guy." And I could have told hir the whole situation, but I didn't. I was trying to stay calm. I was embarrassed. I just said, "He's not dangerous. I don't think."

"You don't *think*," Satya said. "Does he have a gun?"

I didn't know.

Satya said, "Gren, yes, you need the Uzi."

I looked at it. It looked like it was made to take out a battalion. Gordon was just one complicated, selfish, self-loathing man. What was the point of a submachine gun? But I was sure he had secrets. How well did I really know him?

The purse I had brought to hold the gun was too small for the Uzi, so Satya leant me hir backpack—all black, roomy, brand name torn off with a seam ripper. I made sure the Uzi was on "S" before I dropped it to the bottom, gently. The magazine was slotted in and loaded.

"Alright, just bring it back when you're done. Wipe off the fingerprints."

"Thanks, Satya." We hugged for a while. I think ze noticed that I needed the embrace.

I brought the Uzi home to Mischa, who wanted to go shoot it somewhere right away, but I said, "No. I'm going to put it away. Please don't touch it." I put the Uzi back in Satya's backpack and shoved it under Mischa's and my bed, next to empty bags of Cheetos, discarded tissues, and Mischa's rock collection. When I walked out Mischa was pouting. She said, "You're going to let me help with this, right?"

And I said, "Mischa, you know, this is dangerous."

And she said, "Yeah, fucking duh."

So I said, "Mischa, I don't want to see you get in trouble."

To which she replied, "Funny, I could say the same thing about you."

"You just don't need to come, Mischa," I said. "It's a one-person job. I hold up the gun, I stick it in Gordon's face, and then I leave. That's it."

And Mischa said, "Really, and you don't need a driver?"

"No, I can drive."

Mischa said, "Fuck." She said, "Gren, you know, this is my life, too. This could have just as easily been me, finding the means with which to help you. This is my transition, too, Gren. I want to do this. Let me help."

And I thought back to when we first came out, in high school, when the whole world was scary for a million reasons, when I thought, maybe I don't need to do this, be a girl. Well, I was a girl, I guess, but being a girl was endlessly scary. I was the scared one. Mischa said, no, you're going to do this. We're going to do this. It will be okay. And I thought of how scared I was, right then, at that very moment. I thought of having Mischa in the driver's seat as we got away.

"Fine, Mischa," I said, "but I'm holding the gun."

She said okay. And she hugged me, like, yes, we can do this.

Gordon called me the next afternoon, which was a Saturday, to say that the drugs had arrived. Mischa was working and I was in our bedroom, trying to nap. "Yep, I got 'em," he told me. "Your drugs. They're all here."

"That's great, Gordon, sweetie. I'll be over as soon as I can." I was impressed by how confident I sounded calling him sweetie.

"Great," he said. "Don't keep me waiting."

I told him I wouldn't. I walked out to Mischa right then, and without me saying anything, I guess she knew what was up. She hung up on her customer right away—"Calls drop all the time," she said. "What do they know?"—and she put on her sneakers. "Get the gun."

"Get the gun," I said to myself. And then to Mischa, "Okay, let's do this."

"Yep, uh huh," Mischa said, and she waited for me to get the gun, holding the front door open to leave. She got in the driver's seat of my car—she had to remind me to get out my keys—and she started driving, with a jerk, toward the Aloha Motel. I wondered if I would have gotten out of the driveway were it not for Mischa. Mischa asked, "Would you have even gotten out of the driveway if it weren't for me?"

My sister.

She took the back roads, drove with the windows down. It wasn't a long drive, but I wanted her to go more quickly. She seemed to relish in the experience. "We're going to get hormones, Gren. Fuck." But I was still skeptical. I was so worried. I just didn't know. Mischa had this look on her face like, *if anybody fucks with us, I'll kill 'em.* She's always been a fighter, my sister. But it was I that was holding the gun, zipped up in a backpack on my lap. In the side-view mirror, I thought I looked like a panicked hamster. But there was that possibility of the best outcome, which made me smile with Mischa for just a second, because yes, we might get hormones. We might be set. Maybe.

When we got to the motel, I was going to tell Mischa to pull around back, so no one would see us, but I forgot and she parked in the parking lot, just opposite from a new, recently stacked pile of mattresses. I walked across the cracked up shuffleboard court that would one day be a pool—a true jewel, I figured that would be, of the South Florida tourism landscape. I walked right up to Gordon's door with Satya's backpack on my back, and I knocked on Gordon's door three times quickly. *Knock, knock, knock.* "Hey there," Gordon said. "Come on in." I did.

Gordon had Chinese food out on his table, and it was still wrapped, with the receipt taped onto the plastic bag. Gordon started unwrapping it. "Please, Gren," he said. "Sit down. Eat."

I said, "I'm anxious," being honest. "Can you please show me what you got me first?"

And Gordon said, "Yes. Yes, of course. I didn't mean to make you nervous." He walked into his kitchen, which was maybe eight feet from his bed, and he picked up a cardboard box, about the size of a case of wine, that was open and looked like it had been rifled through. I squinted to see what was in it, afraid that it wasn't what I had asked for, and I saw endless paper bags with an unfamiliar pharmacy logo, with what I assumed was Gordon's full name printed in large letters on the top. Gordon Bidet. I thought, okay.

"About the other night," Gordon said, his back still toward me, perhaps from shame. I unzipped the backpack, flipped the Uzi from "S" to "R."

"About the other night," I said, as Gordon turned his head toward the barrel of the Uzi.

He had this look that was hard to read. There was fear, without a doubt. But it wasn't just fear, there was something else—a sadness, I thought. Defeat. I looked at Gordon right then and felt his loneliness. It was filling the room. It was the type of loneliness that comes from being awful to other people. Uncontrollable, persistent loneliness, written on his face with all the fear. The loneliness of hating what you love. He didn't move. He just said, "You fucking faggot."

"Give me the hormones, Gordon. Now." And he did, and I ran out of the room.

I was still holding the Uzi in one hand as I darted across the motel plaza. The cardboard box, overfilled with paper bags, was in the other. Mischa popped the door for me right away, started driving right away, and was on the highway, going toward Satya's house, while I was still in a daze, holding the Uzi. When we had almost arrived, three police cars pulled up behind us and flashed their lights, but just as soon as they had done that, they pulled out past us on the left. Mischa didn't blink. She was perfect, at every step. My sister. She reminded me to wipe the fingerprints off the Uzi in Satya's driveway.

I did, and then we went into Satya's house, where Satya was sitting, smiling, eating oatmeal. "Oatmeal," ze said, "is very good for nervous depression." So we all ate oatmeal. Then we looked closer into the cardboard box, and then we hugged. Because it was all there—a two years' supply of injectable estrogen. A two years' supply of the anti-androgen spironolactone.

Mischa had syringes shipped over from a pen pal in Seattle, who picked them up from a free needle exchange site that was three blocks away from the pen pal's apartment. Mischa took them out, and she explained to me how they work. She warmed up one vial of estrogen valerate in her hands, and she unwrapped one syringe and sucked the liquid up inside. Then she told me to pull down my pants, which I did, and she rubbed an alcohol swab into the upper right-hand quadrant of my buttock. She shot me up, and then I did the same for her. We were both nervous that maybe it wouldn't work, but it did.

We did this every two weeks, sometimes at Satya's house, sometimes at ours. We made a ritual out of it. We tried to keep it special. We cared for each other through our mood swings, and within about three months, we both started feeling it—the increasing softness of our skin, the growing roundness of our hips. That sweet stretching, pinching pain of our swelling nipples. We felt that, and we continued together, growing toward our more genuine lives. We are on those hormones still. They are sustaining us.

Her Hope
Tavner Castle

She would awaken on a colorless hard linoleum after having sat drunk for three days on the roof of a library, reading a book a day. Writing, then forgetting what was being written, eyes tossed into the outer dark, and rambling away into sleep. Stopped when the booze had unfurled a heavy mattress that smothered the senses without comforting the spine. At the border of black-out she would take thin blankets from her pack, her home. With them she would scrub the ground where she could not rise from, so as to remove what made it loathsome...

At bus stops, sudden and oppressed and somehow with more strength then god could subdue, she hid herself behind telephone poles to gulp great schwills of wine like nauseated lighting in an attempt to elevate whatever soul had not been washed away with the rain.

Enraptured with delight by the gift of solitude.
She danced alone to music no other heard.

A music, when exhibited in dance, became sardonic and false with leisure. Her arms would goad her body to follow, and her torso would leap forward causing her legs to trip. And then she was gasping for the breath of air that came with passing cars. Calmed, ruthless within her own monologue. Unable to resonate brevity with the self. The moments of the body became increasingly dictated by forces outside her own design. And so her stomach led her.

Trips to the Salvation Army for lunch and dinner become common. The food is best when it is without flavor. The salad is always too shredded to be eaten with a fork, a spoon is best. The people are watchful, all worried. Some grateful to be eating in a warm place. Other's grateful to be eating at all. And still more who hate to be eating, who curse themselves in their weakness, and hide their shame with anger. Nights of hunks of ground beef served with hot rolls. Nights of shredded bologna inside burnt crusts of cheese served with white bread and gravy that will make an asshole spit relentless fury.

She speaks to few and begins to forget the desire to do so. There was the woman who told her to leave a space of concrete. She sat on her pack smoking a cigarette, then a woman appeared walking down the street like any other. Turning her head in passing and ordaining herself the building's manager, the woman orders the girl to leave shortly. Across the street a few homeless kids play trashy folk music that had all been heard before. People passed them without notice. The building manager swooped back around the corner and began to tell the girl of a parking lot where she could sit when suddenly the girl had an idea and spoke – if you were on the street you'd know why I chose this spot. The women nodded in mid speech and continued walking. And the girl finished her cigarette in peace.

Some days are spent in search of a dry place. Boarded up buildings are probed and prodded, doors are kicked in, nails are upturned from plywood. She stumbles through a door with the thickness of paper into a once garage, a now shooting gallery. The walls were basic concrete blocks, a dollar a piece, there were a hundred and 12 of them. The white paint emitted less presence then the filth that had layered in a corner from too many days, too drunk, too high, too loaded to step outside to piss. The spot chosen for the urinal was under the only window in the room. And the sun had settled white and soothless beyond the mercy of the glass, allowing for the rooms single patch of light. This is where she made herself to sit, with her book, her bottle of wine, her beer, her Fritos, planted beneath the window sill in a garden of filth.

It was cold in the garage. Colder than outside, and how could that be? She wondered, as she disposed of a few loose dirties into a molded blueberry Bolthouse Farm's juice drink. And perhaps, more prominent a question, what was she herself doing there?

In search of the solace of the word.

Out on the bum again after months of sublets. No more rooms that are not her own, she now sleeps in the hard places. A student of some kind. She even appears in the seminars of the local college to listen to lectures on the social consequences of forced sterilization. Hungover and half mad with the absurdity of passing from the whores of Bukowski to the sterile sexuality of Foucault. She sits idle in the warmth of a clean chair and studies the way her professor manages the task of teaching. Students appear to look for the answers to questions on heteronormativity by reciting page numbers. She wonders about her own sexuality. If she will ever be able to shave her legs again, put on a tight dress and wear herself without fear. Those thoughts become managed by hunger, and the need to drink usurps all other boundaries. For, when drunk there is no boundary no fear, no love nor grace. Only oblivion, and the architecture of poverty deciding the course of her life before the day arrives.

Still there is that bit of luck. The bartender who pours the wrong drink and gives out double by mistake. The half pack of Newport Reds found still dry floating in a puddle. A brown box stuffed with a warm burrito and hash browns with cheese. The woman with divine arms embracing her before realizing they were strangers. That one line that makes the whole day worth living.

Then there are the thoughts of a pleasant room. With walls dampened by age, and dust so thick it shines in gashes of light emanating under the shades drawn tight. A private bathroom she will not have to hide inside. She will be sitting on the wood floor, her arms hot pink from a day washing dishes at a dine-n-dive Thai restaurant, its name something to do with Saigon. She will not have much money, no more than she's ever had before, no more than enough. She will be drinking wine tougher than guts bought from the corner store where the clerk never checks her ID. She will be sitting where books and scraps of paper compose a carpet of sorts, and she will not be happy, but she will be content. She will be safe. She will be cooking fried eggs with toast on a cast iron skillet and brewing fresh cowgirl coffee filtered through toilet paper for breakfast.

That is her hope.

MAMA'S HEX
Luna Merbruja

Marla smiles at the scales sprawling over her shoulders. They shine iridescent blues and greens, matching the current color of her eyes. She hones her Shifting as she brushes her afro into thirty-six inches of limp blonde, then wraps her legs tightly with a warm, damp cloth. She needs to meditate for a few minutes while fusing her legs together. Marla imagines her long legs as a mermaid tail, but when she removes the wrap, she reveals a grotesque mashup of bones and fin.

"What is that monstrosity?!?" Liliana retorts, covering her mouth in disgust.

"Trial thirty-eight," Marla grunts, shooting a sharp look at Liliana. "I'm done with this." She pulls her lower mangled body up to her chest and lets her hair fall over like a curtain.

"Your hair is fantastic, and your scales match beautifully with your eyes." Liliana bats her lashes playfully. She is a Shifter mentor for the girl gang, MAMA'S HEX. Liliana is currently in her highly coveted Medusa form, one of the many historical requests from Elites, but her base form is a sun baked rebel that escaped the Administration to become an erotic spy.

She slithers across the room and places her head of serpents near Marla's face. The serpents pull back Marla's hair, gliding soothingly across her face. Marla giggles at the tickling sensation, then raises her face to meet Liliana's eyes.

"A look into these eyes will result in your demise," Liliana teases. Marla's mahogany laughter fills the room for a long moment. "There there, my dear. Shift back for me, please?"

Marla keeps Liliana's stare as her body retracts into human legs. Her scales smooth out into blemish-free night skin. Her hair climbs up into a stormy cloud, her eyes darken to serenity. When Marla's base form is achieved, Liliana kisses her forehead and keeps guard as she sleeps through the night.

It's Marla's first observational night, and Liliana has booked herself an in-house appointment with a low-stakes military officer. She begins decorating the brothel room with pine trees that line the entire space, then carefully focuses the moon's soft lighting onto the corner furthest from the door. Later, Liliana delegates Marla to fix the bed with fresh earth-colored sheets, lubricant, condoms, and dental dams.

Marla pulls the sheets and blankets over the mattress, then tucks the sex supplies under the pillow. Liliana focuses her attention into Shifting. She kneels on all fours, her spine softly cracking and elongating. Her hands crunch inward into paws, and most of her skin begins sprouting thousands of silky hairs. Her face elongates into a muzzle, her eyes brightening to gold. She paces around the room a few times to feel out her new form.

The officer punctually knocks on the door. Liliana quickly stashes Marla in the darkest part of the room with a silencing mask, then paws a lever that unlocks the door. The officer walks in with unsteady legs, his eyes narrowing to make sense of the dark room. He's six feet tall wearing an ironed black button-up shirt, deep blue jeans, and new sneakers. He closes the door behind him with a sweaty palm, his hands shaking.

"Hello?"

Liliana unleashes a low growl, strutting slowly into the light. Her long fur glistens and her honey eyes shine seductively. The officer mouses his way closer to the werewolf. She wags her tail softly against his leg, inviting his touch. He leans down and pets Liliana's coat that feels as soft as feathers. His other hand rubs down her fur to under her belly, to which she responds by submitting to his touch. He straddles her long, hairy body and runs his hands up and down her underside. He grows erect at the sensational pleasure he's experiencing.

"Do you like my soft?" Liliana whispers into his ear.

"Yes, I fuckin' love it." He kisses up her throat.

"Do you want to feel my wet?" She places her paw gently against his throat.

"Yes. Please lemme fuck you," he begs as his flailing hands attempt to unbutton his jeans. He falls onto his hip as the pants tangle around his ankles. Undeterred, he continues to fumble over his clothing until all but his socks remain on his body.

"First, let us move to the bed." She flips over onto all fours and pounces on top of the bed. He joins her on the firm mattress. "Second, slip on protection. It's underneath the pillow." He reaches for the condom, rips it open, and slides it on. "Third, look me in the gold." He peers into her hypnotic eyes, losing sense of all reality. She holds her gaze intensely, growling with hunger. "Now, tell me what you should not. What is the newest weapon you've received?"

"Uhh... sometime last week," he hazily answers. "We all got this retinal upgrade. Yeah, some kind of new scanner tech that lets us see them Trappers when they got them disguises on."

Liliana lowers herself onto his erection, feeling him shudder in pleasure. She coyly digs her toxin-drenched claws into his chest, baring her teeth.

"Elaborate," she demands.

"I dunno what to say. We been huntin' them and tryna find the head bitch in charge. But all we told is to shoot first and don't ask no questions."

Liliana's gaze darts towards Marla's direction.

"Run!" she roars.

Marla jumps out of the corner and dashes to the door. As she reaches for the the lever, bullets pierce through the metal and graze her right arm. Liliana rips the officer's throat out and lunges towards Marla, blood dripping down her jaw. She launches Marla onto her back and leaps out the window, landing gracefully on the roof of the next building. A huge bang! echoes throughout the night as the military rushes into the room. By the time the soldiers look out the window, the Shifters are long gone.

Mama is hunching over Marla with a pair of tweezers in hand. Marla is laid out on the medicine bed, wincing every time Mama meticulously plucks a glass shard out of her skin. Her large hands massage Marla's tender skin, her supple lips meeting the wounds with whispered spells of healing. When she finishes removing the glass, Mama applies a light layer of herbal balm over the open wounds. She stows away the jar of bloodied glass shards for future use.

Marla takes a deep breath. Her eyes watch Mama cross the room to Liliana, still attending to her own wounds.

"Lily, sweetpea, let me see everything."

Liliana bows her head in compliance.

Mama places her palm flat against Liliana's forehead as the eye on the back of her hand opens and projects a memory onto the barren wall. She watches the night play out without making a sound, though her heart jumps at the sight of bullets plummeting the room. She removes her hand and kisses Lily's forehead in appreciation.

"Blessed are we for both of you returning home to me in one piece."

Liliana takes both of Mama's hands into hers, kneeling before her leader. "Mama, you have my sincerest apologies for endangering our dear Marla's life. Please forgive my transgression." She looks up to meet Mama's tearful eyes.

"Honey, you are not at fault for the military's hunt. Please lift your chin and take pride in saving both your lives. I am proud of your bravery."

Mama lifts Liliana to her feet, then embraces her with the loving touch that holds together MAMA'S HEX. "Marla dear, be a doll and call Soon-Ya. It's time we arm ourselves to infiltrate the Administration."

Marla nods her head, feeling conviction boil in her blood. As she picks up the phone, she gazes out the window watching the sunset. To the untrained eye, an eagle flying toward the horizon is just an ordinary bird. To Marla, she sees a sister feeling her freedom.

Lives & Lies
Connifer Candlewood

this unwholesome silence,
wash me out in the sound

our lives and our lies intertwined

the Bird that flies in spite of the storm
a Crab bearing its claws in the shadow of the seagull
Ants in a line lifting their heads in defiance of focused light

well-placed whispers wearing masks under screams

there is so much beauty it can make you cry.

//

Our lives are being divided by the wolves among us. We are
fighting for scraps. We are fighting for nothing. We are fighting
amongst ourselves. Our mirrors reflect an alt-reality. We all live
here. Fuck these people. Fuck my hate. I can't stand these feeds;
how rad-fems and racists are gaining ground in our spaces.
Colored bodies build and die in these movements. A fascist
leader, anti-human laws, mass kidnappings and murders swept
under the rug. We can't give up. However we can, whenever
we can we have to, fight. We must resist with every drop of
our bodies. Until our bones turn to dust we can not stop.

We only have ourselves in this expanding desert.

Elegy

lina corvus

We are in a moment of extreme uncertainty, and I don't know how our future plays out. Things may end happily. Things may go sideways. There's a lot of variance on the road ahead. And if everything does go worst case scenario, if I do end up killed by right-wing neo-nazis, the machinery of the state, or a nuclear weapon, it might help to tell you who I am while I still can. Before my voice is silenced.

I am a trans woman. I knew I was wrong as a kid, but I didn't have the words to explain how. When I learned those words, I used them to break the shackles of a gender that had been assigned to me, and I got to be who, and what, I really am. I regret one or two things in my life, but I have never regretted being true to *who* I am. And that's still true, even if I have to die for *what* I am.

I am queer, kinked, and not particularly monogamous. I have found love. I have spent ten wonderful years with a woman who feels similarly, and should the world continue on, I hope to have many more. But love is an exploration. Connection with another is one of the most wonderful experiences a person can have, and I would strongly advise that you try it. So long as you're open and honest with the people you love, connection does not need to be zero sum.

I am a Quaker, a religious pacifist with reverence for the truth. I believe there is the goddess in each of us, and that is the spark of life. Life is the goddess, and life is inherently valuable to me. I will not willingly bend a knee to any creed that empowers its followers to commit violence. I fear that I will have to prove the sincerity of my beliefs in the times ahead, and I hope that I live up to who I think I am. Because for me, life is valuable, and I fear I may end up having to fight for it. I fear that love alone may not save us.

I am an analyst and a writer. I interpret criminal justice data for an organization that helps get people out of the brutal jails and prisons in our nation, and instead gives them opportunities to have their needs met and to succeed. Justice is not about penalty; it is about making a community whole again. Certainty and celerity of punishment are far more effective deterrents than severity of sentence, and yet our legal system has adopted a severity-based model of deterrence. It is cruel, and I work alongside it to divert as many people as we can to more progressive paths. I have helped save people, and I am proud of the work that I do.

I am an activist. I have made change in the world, albeit quietly. I have stood up for what is right, even at personal cost. I hope I do so again, because it is important to stand when you can and others can't. I bear the scars of these battles, but in my mind and not my body. It is not the only trauma I've endured, and yet I am still here.

I live a moral life, and I am happy. The right-wing propaganda down the line may portray me and mine as some miserable deviants who lived as outcasts. This is how people like me are typically written out of history. But it is untrue. I have had opportunities to do blessed things, I have been close with a great number of amazing people, and I have had a world's worth of pleasurable experiences. I would do it all again in an instant, and perhaps, right before the very end, I will do so.

Even if I should perish, my words will live on. May my life, may my joys, provide another trans person hope in the future. There is good in this world, and we trans folk are part of that good.

Ode

Joss Barton

Our humanity is a burden on the soft strains of death. What time's the funeral? I sit here handcuffed and led through halls peeling with pale yellow paint. Welcome to the present awful sum of oppression! Hear the familiar voice of violence rising! Feel the strength of our outrage! Caress it as if it were your own life you had to battle for in blood. The years of unfulfilled longing echo in rings carved in flesh and bone. It speaks through the voice of little girls begging for beauty.

WE WON'T BE NICE. WE WILL SCREAM AND HOLLER AND BREAK SHIT UNTIL OUR SISTERS ARE FREE AND SAFE FROM THE GAZE OF MEN WHO WOULD RATHER KILL US THAN SHARE US WITH THE WORLD!

We hear civilized languages debase our humanity. We watch the cultural exorcisms of transgender women on the streets of New York and New Orleans. We see ourselves disappearing behind the white swinging door of EQUALITY. I stopped believing in god the day I heard my Sunday school teacher justify why the Israelites had to commit genocide against the children of Canaan and I stopped believing in American Democracy the morning I saw the body of Michael Brown beneath an August sky. Did a surge of love and compassion sweep through his veins as he bled out on warm asphalt? Did he moan something awful as he thought of how sons wear on a mother like the scars on her skin from sunburns or the cheap hair dyes she buys from the drugstore down the street to color away the gray and the grief from her brittle roots. Or was all this replaced by a swift, seething anger as his soul seeped into the earth to possess and haunt it with the rotting stench of white loathing. Welcome to the dark phases of womanhood of never havin' been a girl. Of never havin' the world lift you up in femme glory. Of never feelin' the protection of daddy's arms or momma's blush.

I'm in St. Louis the morning I hear that Penny Proud was murdered. Less than forty-eight hours earlier I was walking through the French Quarter in black patent leather pumps drunk on vodka and beer. I'm wearing a tan abstract rainbow print dress that reminds me of technicolor wood grain. We eat brunch and I spend too much money at an overpriced hipster cafe on blue crab hash to pretend I'm not a poor queer. I swallow clear distilled grains spiked with tonic water and cranberry juice on upstairs, outdoor patios with drunk faggots on a Sunday afternoon. I tip a few dollars to a transgender drag queen with tan tits in a mod spandex bodysuit and pumped lips. We revel in ignorance and bliss down Bourbon Street as I stop every few hours to retuck my dick and balls into my ass.

Two nights before, as we sat in a taxi drifting us down disheveled streets toward The Phoenix, the driver tells me that the GURLS gather near a lonely green lit bar on the corner, that they can pick up a DATE here if they need to make some cash, and that I could find myself a man in need of a peculiar type of woman. I'm wearing a black spaghetti strap dress with a blue and black leopard print shawl. My lips are dark red and my legs are wrapped in black-back-seam pantyhose to match my black lacquer stilettos. We continue to the leather bar, and on the second floor where the lights are off and the men play in secluded cubbies, a man asks if he can buy the pretty lady a drink.

—DID HE JUST CALL YOU A LADY?!!!! [INSANE LAUGHTER]

—Yes, he did!

—He must be fucking blind! Cause you ain't no damn lady!

—Fuck you WHORE!

I take the glass dripping with vodka and soda from the shirtless, middle-aged cub and smile as I walk toward the white man at the end of the bar. He looks like a textbook illustration of a forty-year-old computer programmer with wire glasses, tan cargo pants, and a plain t-shirt. He asks me where I live. I tell him Saint Louis.

We chat about Ferguson and Michael Brown and the Police State residing in my hometown. He rubs his hands on my thighs and my ass. I smile and drink another cocktail.

The second floor bar is dark and the bartender tells me I can't leave the bar.

—I'm sorry darlin' but the dark rooms are for MEN only.

The next day brings a cream sun dress, nude pumps, and a brown and blue reptile head band. We walk around The French Quarter and meet up with an old college friend. He sits at a Quarter queer bar in a turquoise Lacoste polo sipping a beer. We embrace in hugs as I introduce him to my friends from Saint Louis. The night becomes a dark blur as we stroll from bar to bar sucking liquor from straws and I tell my old peer my desire to become a woman. He sounds honest in his support of my identity and, in my drunken haze, I latch onto his understanding and plead for him to fuck my pussy.

Sometime during this blackout, Penny was brushing her hair. She might have been painting her nails. She could have been on the same street laughing or singing or dancing as gold rays burned down the aisles of Cajun streets. I may have seen the shadow of her ass behind a graffiti corner as I tried to balance vodka-soaked knees on black heels. I may have heard her scream into the night as I kissed the lips of bourbon-burned gay boys. I may have summoned her, as I speak these words into the silent air of a cold night.

—I NEED TO FEEL ABANDONED. I NEED TO FEEL LOVED. I NEED TO FEEL LOST. PLEASE FUCK ME DADDY! FILL MY ASS WITH YOUR CUM! FORGET ME AND BREED ME! GIVE ME A REASON TO KEEP THE POISON INSIDE MY EYES AS THE WORLD TRIES TO ERASE ME. MY BREASTS SWELL WITH THE PAIN OF HUMAN EXISTENCE, AND I CUM LIKE THE POURING RAIN EACH TIME YOU CALL MY NAME! TELL ME YOU CAN'T STOP YOURSELF FROM LOVING ME. TEAR ME UP.

Index of Content Warnings

Black, Trans, and Still Breathing
KOKUMO
CW: slavery, violence, genocide,
religion, transphobia, deadly weapons

Before They Were Flesh
Magpie Leibowitz
CW: death

Weekend
Casey Plett
CW: addiction, ED, body shame, hard drugs,
internalized transmisogyny, sex work

1 AM
Ana Valens
CW: body dysphoria, chemical dependency

Mosca's Last Ride
Sascha Hamilton
CW: white supremacy, anti-abortionist
propaganda, violence, depression, suicide

Holy Love
Talia C. Johnson
CW: internalized transmisogyny, dysphoria

Wednesday Morning, 7:26 am
erica, inchoate
CW: expression of internalized transmisogyny
toward narrator, mentions of sexual assault

Disabled
Ariel Howland
CW: ableism

Burdens
Oti Onum
CW: extreme poverty, police state

The Most Important Trans Woman I Never Knew
Lilith Dawn
CW: internalized transmisogyny

Her Name was Pearl
Sophia Quartz
CW: psychological child abuse, suicide attempt,
transmisogyny, heavy feelings

Moments of the Forgotten while Surviving
Connifer Candlewood
CW: physical and psychological child abuse, dysphoria

Father
Lawrence Walker III
CW: psychological child abuse, transmisogyny

My Father's Stench was Stronger than His Fist
Oti Onum
CW: physical and psychological child abuse, dysphoria

Behind Enemy Lines
Ariel Howland
CW: physical and psychological child abuse,
racism, transphobia, discussion of suicide

Girlhood, Interrupted
Amy Heart
CW: intense depiction of body dysphoria, transmisogyny

Usefulness or Filthiness
AR Mannylee Rushet
CW: explicit suicidal ideology, masochism

Coastlines
Sara Oliver Wight
CW: child abuse, smoking, alcohol

Godless Rose
Lillita Lustre
CW: mental illness

Read to Me
Tyler Vile
CW: discussion of cannibalism, smoking, depression

Night of the Dead Lesbians
Bridget Liang
CW: violence, smut, misogyny, revenge fantasy

Goldilocks Lynched
Lawrence Walker III
CW: violence, depictions of anti-blackness

*Being a Non Male/Non Female Person in the Literary
World, Written in the Form of a Dream*
Moss Angel
CW: mutilation, dysphoria

Broke Pieces
AR Mannylee Rushet
CW: violence, depression

GAUNT
Luna Merbruja
CW: codependency, mutilation

I don't think you understand what 'attraction' means
Tobi Hill-Meyer
CW: sex, transmisogyny

Failure
Larissa Glasser
CW: death of a loved one, alcohol, suicide, suicidal ideation

Hormones
Serafima Mintz
CW: sex work, mention of sexual abuse, deadly
weapons, needles, incarceration, transmisogyny

Her Hope
Tavner Castle
CW: extreme poverty, alcohol, and drug use

MAMA'S HEX
Luna Merbruja
CW: violence, sex work, transformation, deadly weapons

Lives & Lies
Connifer Candlewood
CW: radical feminism, racism, fascism

Ode
Joss Barton
CW: alcoholism, sex, transmisogyny,
systemic violence, murder

Heartspark Staff

Amy Heart • *Executive Publisher*

Amy Heart is a queer storyteller and social justice advocate, dedicated to lifting the voices of trans girls and trans women everywhere.

From 2002 to 2013, Amy worked exclusively in non-profit community television as both educator and community organizer. Since then, she has focused her energy on 'unlearning' white supremacy, studying disability justice, building strong relationships with other trans women artists, and helping people become fluent in modern technology. Amy has a Bachelor's of Fine Arts in Film Studies from the University of California, Santa Barbara, and currently resides in her "chosen" hometown of Olympia, Washington.

Sugi Pyrrophyta • *Editor*

Sugi works against the hegemony that academic institutions have on knowledge and that financial institutions have on power, specifically the roles that capital and obedience to oppressive structures play in upholding/withholding those institution and the rewards. She has been working most of her life on collecting stories of the lived experience of those most oppressed while attempting to make impossible the powers that hold us down. She knows first-hand and viscerally how hard it is to carve out time/energy to create while fighting every step for her and her friends' survival, and has no further accolades to dress herself in here because *you can do anything, you don't need a fancy degree or an income or to have been published before; you are the fire that keeps us warm.*

Larissa Glasser • *Editor*

Larissa Glasser is a librarian and queer trans woman genre writer from Boston.

Her debut novella *F4* (2018) is available from Eraserhead Press. Her Twitter is @larissaeglasser

Serafima Mintz • *Copyeditor*

Serafima Mintz teaches reading and comprehension in Palm Beach County, Florida. She has been published in *Gertrude* and *the Fine Print,* and she writes the zine *Even Noisy Sparrows.* To contact Serafima, email her at *serafima.mintz@gmail.com.*

Mia Rose Elbo • *Cover Artist*

Mia is a trans and lesbian creator from Santiago de Chile.

As a digital communications and new media graduate with vast work experience in digital marketing agencies and IT companies, Mia is looking to take up on new challenges and opportunities to use her skills and experience for good rather than for big corporations profit. She has a deep interest for positive representation and tries her best to make trans people visible individuals in her country. Mia loves drawing, food, and musicals. When she's not doing photoshoots, giving talks or interviews, she likes to play games and watch movies with her wife and two kittens.

Bridget Liang • *Consulting Director*

Bridget Liang is a mixed race, queer, transfeminine, neurodiverse, disabled, fat fangirl.

They came into their queerness in Hamilton Ontario and co-founded RADAR Youth Group at the LGBTQ Wellness Centre (the Well), the first queer group in a high school in Hamilton, and were instrumental in the passing of an equity policy at at HWDSB. Bridget is a budding academic, community researcher, workshop and group facilitator, performance artist, and writer. Much of their work revolves around intersectionality and arts-based research. Check out their blog at *https://bridgetliang.wordpress.com*.

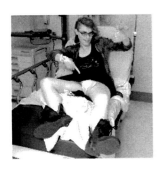

Evelyn Yaussy • *Creative Director*

Evelyn is a death metal loving trans lesbian living with her super hot, gay, art wife in Olympia.

Originally a Chicago area filmmaker crafting everything from video poetry to documentary film from as early as the age of six, she continues her work in the Pacific Northwest by creating meaningful space for herself and other trans individuals desirous of actualizing their A/V dreams. Before graduating Chicago's largest & second-most-bullshit art school (suck it Art Institute), Columbia College, she and fellow activists forced the administration to the negotiating table and successfully rewrote the sexual assault policy to favor student survivors instead of college lawyers. She's spent the better part of the last couple of years escaping hippy cultist terfs in Oregon and working to build and support the Heartspark collective.

Hey, Writers! Do you want help publishing?

Look up our upcoming projects and learn more about Heartspark Press at *hearstparkpress.com.*

Also, you can email us at *hello@heartsparkpress.com.*

Check out our Oral Storytelling Project at *heartspark.bandcamp.com.*

CPSIA information can be obtained
at www.ICGtesting.com
Printed in the USA
LVOW10*1211100118

562476LV00002B/4/P

9 780692 951088